ABBY

Calamity
and
Chaos

Margaret Ryan

Hodder
Children's
Books

a division of Hodder Headline Limited

To Jenny,
with love and thanks for all her help.

It was the start of another ordinary day: the plop of letters on the mat, the smell of toast on the grill, the sound of Mum yelling at me to get up for school. I got up eventually, looked in the mirror and did a spot check. Yesterday's giant zit was still there, beaming at me, despite zapping it with three times the recommended amount of zit cream. I would write to the manufacturers after school and demand my money back. I was just composing a curt letter in my head and struggling into my school skirt when I noticed it: the silence. Usually Mum is like the speaking clock in the morning. Or the nagging clock. You know the kind of thing . . .

'It is now eight o'clock, Abby. You will miss the bus.'

'It is now ten past eight, Abigail. You will definitely miss the bus.'

'It is now twenty past eight, Abigail Montgomery, and if you think I am going to run you to school you are very much mistaken.'

the nagging clock was silent. Something was
..ong. Why had Mum stopped? Had she run away
from home? Was she ill? Was she lying in a pool of
blood on the kitchen floor? Was there a mad axe-
murderer in the house? I switched off what Mrs
Jackson, my English teacher, calls my over-fertile
imagination, picked up a cricket bat, and went
downstairs to find out.

Mum was in the kitchen with a letter in her hand
and a curiously stunned expression on her face.

'What is it?' I asked, ditching the cricket bat as
the mad axe-murderer was nowhere to be seen.

Mum made a small gulping noise.

I did a mental check. Could the letter be from
school? Had I done anything recently to merit it?
Hmm . . .

. . . I was a bit rude about Ms Hale's flowery
knickers being on show at netball practice . . . and
I may have pinged a few peas at Belinda Fishcake
Fisher in the dining hall when she was going on
about how lucky she was NEVER EVER to get spots
. . . but nothing serious.

Mum still didn't answer. She just stood there,
letter in one hand, half-eaten toast in the other.

'Earth to Mother,' I intoned. 'Are you receiving
me? One nod for yes, two nods for no, three nods
and you can leave your law firm and get a job in a
nodding dog factory.'

Mum looked at me like I'd just got off the last
bus from the planet Moron – a look I knew well.

'Your grandma's coming to stay in two weeks' time,' she said.

'What?' My mouth hung open like Danny Plover's in Three B. Everyone reckons he must have evolved from a dogfish. 'You mean Grandma Aphrodite?'

Mum gave me another of her looks.

'Well, it can't be your other gran unless the afterlife has a postal service.'

Ooh, sarky socks. And she complains about my smart mouth.

Mum handed me the letter then proceeded to tell me what was in it. Like I hadn't learned to read in Year One.

'She's sold the sheep farm in Australia, and wants to come back here and stay for a while to get to know you better.'

'Cool,' I said. I hadn't seen Grandma since I was three, more than a decade ago.

'It's not cool,' said my mother. 'It is anything but cool. You don't know what your grandmother is like. She's untidy, airy-fairy, selfish and disruptive.'

Ace. I liked her already and couldn't wait for her to arrive.

I ate a hasty breakfast of rabbit pooh. It's a ghastly concoction Mum makes up. She buys organic everything; oats, nuts and raisins etc. She insists I eat it because it's good for me. Personally I'd prefer a large KitKat and a Coke. I grabbed my rucksack, flew out of the house and caught the school bus by the skin of my train-tracked teeth. Braces are a fashion statement, right? Wrong. If I didn't wear them I would be Goofy's double. Spots *and* horizontal teeth. How could Mother Nature have got it so wrong?

I was just pondering this (ponder – to consider carefully – is my latest word, by the way. I collect words. I know, I know, WEIRDO. I don't care. There will be more words later) when I sat down in the only empty seat. Unfortunately it was beside Belinda Fishcake. She sprang away from me like I had PLAGUE tattooed on my forehead.

'You've got something in your hair,' she cried. 'I hope it's not catching!'

I pulled a strand of auburn hair down in front of my face and looked cross-eyed at it.

'Nope,' I said. 'It's a bit of soggy rabbit pooh I was saving for later.' And I slid it off and ate it.

'I can't believe you did that,' said an appalled Belinda.

Neither could I. But it's all Fishcake's fault. She brings out the worst in me. There I was, sitting in my crumpled uniform and odd socks while she was little Miss Perfect, from the top of her gleaming blonde head to the tips of her designer trainers. Not a hair out of place, not a spot on her face. And her bosom was already bigger than mine would probably ever be. Mother Nature had got it wrong all right.

Belinda smoothed down her already crease-free skirt and preened.

'You look like you slept in that uniform,' she said.

'I have more important things to concern myself with than mere appearance,' I said loftily. 'For a start, I've been busy preparing for my famous grandmother, Aphrodite, coming from Australia.'

'Aphrodite,' frowned Belinda. 'Wasn't she the Greek goddess of love?'

'And beauty,' I said. I knew because I'd looked it up.

Belinda gave a loud, rather unladylike, snort.

'She didn't pass that on then, did she?'

I was haughty. 'True beauty comes from within,' I informed her, and for the rest of the journey I rattled on about Grandma. I endowed her with as many good qualities and fantastic adventures as my fertile imagination could come up with. I was just about to mention the shark wrestling when we got to school.

'Well,' sniffed Belinda Fishcake. 'I can't wait to meet your grandma. I bet she tells even taller tales than you do.'

'Just wait and see,' I said, and crossed my fingers. Me and my big mouth.

But it wasn't as big as Belinda's. By the end of the day everyone in my class knew about Grandma Aphrodite, including Mrs Jackson.

'Your grandma sounds a very interesting character,' she said to me during English. 'I do hope I'll get the chance to meet her.'

'Oh yes,' I said. 'I expect you will.' And I crossed my fingers again. What had I let Grandma in for?

At home, Grandma was my main topic of conversation for the next two weeks. What did she look like? Was she like Mum? Was she fat or thin? Tall or short? Grandma had sent us photographs over the years, but she was no great shakes as a photographer. In fact, I think she *had* the shakes, for most of the photos were out of focus, and those that weren't had heads or feet missing.

But Mum didn't really answer my questions, except to say wait and see. So I waited.

3

As Grandma's arrival approached Mum got herself in a total panic. She turned the house upside down, cleaning and polishing.

'What is the point of tidying up,' I said, 'if Grandma is so untidy she's just going to mess it up again?'

'Because I shall know it was tidy in the first place,' said Mum.

'Illogical, Captain,' I said, in my Mr Spock voice, but she was too busy dusting inside the teapot to hear.

She did draw the line at tidying my room, though. In fact she drew the line at entering my room. It may be on account of the CAUTION – DANGEROUS WASTE notice I posted on the door, but more likely because last time she came in, she skidded on the buttered toast I had left lying on the floor, and ended up in Casualty with a sprained wrist.

I had to do the shopping for weeks after that. I

didn't mind. Goodbye rabbit pooh. Hello KitKats.

On the day Grandma was due I made her a Welcome Home poster and stuck it up above her bed in the spare room. I put a cuddly koala on the bedside chair to make her feel really at home. Grandma had sent me the koala when I was little. It had been up in the loft for a while, but still played *Waltzing Matilda* if you turned the key in its back, though one of its front paws leaked sawdust where the mice had got at it. Still, it's the thought that counts.

Finally it was time to go and meet Grandma at the station. She had phoned Mum when she landed at Heathrow and told her what train she would be on. Mum and I drove to the station, Mum not saying very much and me chattering nineteen to the dozen. I didn't stop till we were standing on the station platform, waiting for Grandma to get off the train.

Lots of people got off and I imagined where they'd all been. Trekking in the jungle? Visiting a space station? Meeting the Queen? Some carried large briefcases, so they had probably just been away on business. Boring. But though I looked at all the women of Grandma's age, there was no Grandma. After a few minutes the platform was empty, except for an empty crisp packet blowing in the wind.

Mum's face was anxious. Anxious and angry.

'That's just typical,' she muttered. 'Your grandma misses the train and doesn't even bother to let us know . . .'

She was just about to turn on her heel when the guard's van opened and Grandma got out. I knew it was Grandma from the stunned expression on Mum's face.

'Mum?' she said, faintly.

'Grandma?' I asked.

Grandma Aphrodite looked up and spotted us.

'G'day, girls,' she yelled and rushed over and enveloped us in a great bear hug. Or rather a great sheep hug, because despite the warm weather, Grandma was wearing a smelly old sheepskin jacket. But, worse than that, on her sizeable feet she wore real crocodile-skin boots.

'I had to travel in the guard's van,' she said, 'because the other passengers complained about the smell of old Belle here,' and she indicated her sheepskin jacket. 'They seemed to think she ponged a bit. But I didn't want to be parted from her so we travelled with the parcels and an anaconda called Fred. Nice chap. Didn't say much. But hey, it's great to see you both. Abby, you're a real beauty. Much prettier than your photographs.'

I really liked her. She didn't say, 'My, how you've grown,' which considering I was three years old the last time she saw me, was pretty good. Nor did she ask how I was getting on at school. Why is it adults only have these two topics of conversation when they meet children? Why don't they ever ask who your favourite pop group is, or if you'd like an ice cream?

But Grandma was heading back to the train.

'I'll just get my trunk,' she said, 'and we'll go home and get acquainted again.'

She squeaked back to the train in her crocodile boots and came back lugging a huge trunk.

'The rest of my luggage will follow on later. Now where are your wheels?'

I looked at Mum. She was wearing that dazed expression again. I looked at Grandma. She was all smiles. These two seemed so different, yet they were mother and daughter. Hmm, I thought, life was about to become very interesting. Very interesting indeed.

4

When we got home, the first thing Mum did was hang Grandma's sheepskin jacket out on the washing line.

'Won't do any good, Eva,' said Grandma. 'Old Belle smelled bad while she was alive – she isn't going to change now she's dead.'

Mum ignored her and took some fabric spray outside to give old Belle a good squirt.

I took my chance to have a word with Grandma. She'd become very Australian over the last ten years. Very open and friendly and straightforward. So I asked her a straightforward question about the crocodile boots.

'Don't you know it's wrong to kill animals for their skins?' I said. 'Don't they know about conservation in Australia?'

'Of course,' said Grandma. 'But with this particular croc it was more about preservation. Preserving the life of my dear husband, Handsome Harris. Did your mum tell you about him?'

I nodded sympathetically. 'She said he had a heart attack and died.'

Grandma laughed. 'A heart attack and died? Trust Eva to tidy things up. She was always tidying things up, even as a child. Drove me mad. No, Handsome Harris didn't have a heart attack. He got roaring drunk one night and fell into the sheep dip. That's what happened to Handsome Harris.'

Grandma's eyes grew misty. 'I do miss him, but while I've got old Belle and the crocodile boots there's still a bit of Handsome Harris with me. See, old Belle was his favourite sheep. Handsome raised her from a lamb after her mum was killed in a storm. She became a pet. She always had her dinner with us and slept at the foot of the bed. She didn't really know she was a sheep – probably thought she was just a woolly human being. When she finally went belly up Handsome made her into a jacket for me, so old Belle would still be around. Around me, at any rate.'

'OK,' I said, slightly mollified. 'But what about the crocodile boots? You didn't keep a croc at the end of the bed?'

'No,' grinned Grandma, 'Handsome was paddling upriver one day looking for some lost sheep when a large croc bit a hole in his boat. Bit a hole in his leg too, and was going for the rest of him, but Handsome had other ideas. He'd been a prize wrestler in his youth and the old croc got more than he bargained for.

Handsome made me the boots out of the skin. Waste not, want not, he always said, though I was never keen on the teeth round the top. What do you think?'

'Gross,' I said.

Grandma nodded. 'You can take recycling a bit too far.'

At that moment the back door banged open and Mum came in with the empty tin of fabric freshener and put it in the bin.

'Told you it wouldn't do any good, Eva,' said Grandma. 'Looks like you're stuck with the smell of old Belle.'

'Only till you find your own place,' said Mum, rather rudely I thought, considering Grandma had only just got here.

'Yes, well, naturally,' said Grandma, clearing her throat and looking as shifty as I do when I've been caught scoffing the last chocolate biscuit.

Mum knew that look.

'You are going to get a place of your own?'

'Yes, well, naturally, of course, in the fullness of time . . .' said Grandma.

'But you said in your letter that with the money from the sale of the sheep farm . . .'

'Yes, well . . .' Grandma looked shifty again. 'That was before I knew about the debts. Handsome Harris wasn't very good at book-keeping or paying bills or taxes or anything like that. He left the finances in a bit of a mess.'

Mum sighed. 'I might have guessed. How much money have you got?'

Mum was nothing if not direct, but Grandma didn't seem to mind.

'About ten,' she said.

'Well, ten thousand will be enough for a deposit on a small flat.'

Grandma Aphrodite shook her head sadly. 'Not ten thousand, Eva,' she said. 'Ten pounds.'

Mum's shoulders drooped and she sank down on to the sofa.

'I knew it,' she said. 'I knew it the minute your letter arrived. I knew that there would be trouble.'

'No trouble, Eva,' Grandma beamed. 'I can take some of the weight off your shoulders. I can help you around the house. I can tidy up.'

Mum looked at Grandma's trunk cluttering up the tiny hall, the crocodile boots sitting on the coffee table, and all the neighbourhood cats roaming the garden, attracted by the smell of old Belle, and drooped even more.

'And I can make a mean beef stew,' added Grandma helpfully.

My strictly vegetarian mother closed her eyes in disbelief.

I grinned. It looked like Grandma Aphrodite was here to stay. But Mum needed time to recover. It was time to exit stage left.

'Come on, Grandma,' I said. 'I'll help you unpack.'

Apart from being my usual helpful self, I couldn't help wondering what was in that trunk. It wasn't quite big enough for a body, but I suppose if the body was doubled up or even chopped up . . . It couldn't be Handsome Harris in there, could it? Nah, Grandma'd never have got him through customs. Still, she never did say what she did with him . . . Recycled him? Surely not. I had a quick look at what else Grandma was wearing, but none of it looked like it could have come from a handsome Australian. But there was only one way to find out. I put my over-active imagination away and went to help open the trunk.

#

There was no dead body in the trunk, but something equally interesting. Vintage clothes. Grandma hoarded everything. She had all her old school photographs, and all the clothes she ever wore when she was a teenager in the sixties. I lifted out loads of minidresses and miniskirts and held them against me.

'Were they really the "Swinging Sixties", Grandma?' I asked. I had seen a TV programme once about the 'old days'.

'Oh yes,' said Grandma. 'We thought we could do anything. We thought we could change the world. We thought we were invincible.'

'Invincible,' I said. 'Good word. I'll add it to my collection.'

Then I tried on Grandma's collection of old clothes. They fitted perfectly, especially the little minidresses and the white, stretchy, knee-high boots.

'You know, Abby,' grinned Grandma, 'With

the right pale foundation and black eye make-up you could be me. You look just like I did back then.'

I looked at myself in the long mirror in Grandma's room and sure enough I could have stepped out of an old movie.

I went to show Mum.

'What do you think?' I said. 'Do I look like Twiggy? Grandma says she was a famous model in the sixties. Maybe I should think about modelling as a career. I'm skinny enough.'

Mum looked up from the vegetarian lasagne she was making for supper. Her face had on its 'I'm doing my best to be patient' expression.

'You'll get your A levels and have a proper career, young lady. Don't let your grandma fill your head with any more nonsense; there's more than enough there already!'

All this for trying on a frock!

I opened my mouth to protest, but Mum was in full flow.

'And if you two are quite finished playing, I would appreciate some help with dinner. The table will not set itself and the milk's gone sour.'

But not as sour as you, I *thought* about saying, but didn't. Instead I gave my usual shrug which annoys Mum even more, got out the place mats and began to set the table.

Dinner started off pretty well. Grandma and I were on our best behaviour. We chatted about

Australia, about the Sydney Opera House, about Ayers rock, about the sheep farm, and Grandma remembered her manners and said how nice the home-made tomato soup was. That always pleases Mum. Not to be outdone, I said how nice the lasagne was. Grandma agreed, and all would have been well if she hadn't added . . .

'But you couldn't feed a man on just veggies in the outback, Eva. They'd go belly up in two days without some good red meat.'

Mum looked stony-faced.

'It may have escaped your notice, Mother,' she said, in her cool little courtroom voice, 'but we are not in the outback. Nor are there any men present.'

'Oh, I noticed,' said Grandma, quite unperturbed. 'Especially about the men. Why don't you have a man, Eva? You used to fancy men. You haven't gone funny in your old age, have you?'

Mum's stony face turned pink.

'No, I haven't,' she said. 'Not that it's any of your business. I don't have time for any of that. I'm too busy earning a living and looking after my daughter.'

'Hmm,' said Grandma, unconvinced. 'But what do you do about sex?'

Mum turned brick red.

'That's certainly none of your business,' she spluttered, 'and not a suitable subject to bring up in front of a child.'

I looked round about me.

'There's no child present,' I said.

'Abigail,' yelled Mum. 'Go to your room.'

I sighed and got up from the table.

'It's not fair,' I said. 'This always happens. Just when it looks like something interesting might be talked about. How am I supposed to learn about things if you don't talk about them!'

But the subject was dropped. I know because I closed my bedroom door with a bang then opened it again quietly and listened . . .

I didn't find out anything I didn't know already. I already knew my dad had gone off, never to be seen again, when he realized Mum was pregnant. And I knew that my grandad, Grandma Aphrodite's first husband, had died and she'd gone off to Australia on holiday some years later and had met Handsome Harris.

'I didn't think you needed me,' I could hear Grandma saying. 'You seemed so organized with Abby, and so certain of what you were doing. Now I'm not so sure. Not so sure at all. Perhaps it's as well I'm back to look after my daughter.'

I strained forward to hear Mum's reply, and the door swung open and creaked loudly.

'Abigail,' shouted Mum. 'Stop listening at the door and go to bed.'

I gave a couple of snorts and a loud snore and pretended to be already asleep, but I don't think Mum was convinced.

I got ready for bed and thought about the day's

events. Grandma had only been here five minutes and already life was much livelier.

What else will happen? I wondered.

I didn't have too long to wait to find out.

6

Grandma soon settled in. 'As happy as a maggot on a sheep's backside,' she said.

Mum shuddered. She's not good with anything creepy crawly. I have to remove the spiders from the bath for her.

Old Belle had been relegated to the garden shed and the crocodile boots to the cupboard under the stairs where the Hoover lurked. But the house would never be the same again. Our quiet, ordered existence had changed for ever. It was great. For a start, Grandma drank beer straight from the bottle. Glasses were for wimps. The beer made her even more chatty and she told stories of her schooldays. Like when Grandma had dropped her school bag down the high stairwell for a dare, hit the caretaker and nearly got expelled. Or when she was caught singing rude words to the Christmas carols in church and was thrown out of the school choir.

I loved the stories, but Mum was not amused.

'Don't encourage Abby to misbehave,' she

sniffed. 'She has to work hard at school to pass her exams.'

'Oh, she'll be right,' said Grandma, giving me a wink and whispering, 'I'll teach you the rude words to *Good King Wenceslas* later.'

I smiled. I knew some already, but maybe Grandma's were even ruder.

When Mum was out at work and I was out at school, Grandma forgot all about the tidying up and got to know the neighbours instead.

'Did you know old Mrs Polanski at number fourteen has to go into hospital soon with her bunions, and has no one to look after her dog? I just said to her "No worries, Mrs P – we'll look after Benson." Is that OK?'

'No, it is not OK,' seethed Mum. 'Her dog's a huge great beast. He chases the postman and is always scratching. He's probably got—'

'Fleas,' said Grandma. 'I think he has. But I'll buy him a flea collar. He'll be right.'

'I wish you wouldn't keep saying everything will be right. Everything is not all right.'

'You want me to tell that poor old worried woman, who's going into hospital to have her feet bones mashed up, that we can't help her in her hour of need? You want me to tell her that we can't help out a neighbour in trouble?'

Grandma definitely had a way with words.

Mum glared and flounced out of the room.

Grandma grinned. 'Looks like we've got ourselves

a pet for a little while, Abby. Can't stand a house without pets.'

I grinned back. Grandma had managed in a few days what I'd been nagging on about for years.

I was just thinking about this in English next day and planning the walks I would take Benson on when Mrs Jackson handed out our next assignment.

'For next week,' she said, 'I want you to prepare a three-minute talk. It can be on any subject you like. You will come out to the front of the room and deliver it to the rest of the class. Try to make it as interesting as you can. We don't want anyone falling asleep!'

Someone at the back immediately gave a loud snore.

'I know what I'm going to talk about,' said Belinda Fishcake as soon as the bell for next lesson rang. 'Beauty therapy. That's what I'm going to study when I leave school.'

'I'm going to talk about tiger moths,' said Will Struthers. 'I saw them at an air show.'

'Ooh, I hate the way moths flutter,' squeaked Belinda and fluttered her eyelashes.

'He means the old planes, idiot,' I said.

'Well, Miss Know-it-all,' Belinda sniffed, 'let's see what *you* have to talk about. Will it be "Learn to Love Your Zits" or "One Hundred and One Ways With Lavatory Brush hair"?'

I could cheerfully have grabbed her by her shiny

blonde hair and swung her into orbit, but instead I gritted my teeth and smiled sweetly. No mean feat!

'Just wait and see,' I said. 'Just wait and see.'

7

I suppose I should tell you a bit about my school. Not that it will be much different from yours. Cosgrove High is an old school. The original building's grey stone, covered in ivy that tries to grow in through the windows in the summer. I spend most of my time in a wooden hut in the playground. There are three huts – or stalags as we call them. They're too hot in summer and freezing in winter. Most of my classes are in stalag three. I sit at the back of the room near the window. That way I can keep an eye on what's going on. The school's still buzzing about who sneaked the vodka into the slush puppy machine at the end of last term. Everyone kept going back to the hall for refills at lunchtime, and afternoon school was very merry. Mr Doig, the head teacher, had a severe word with us at final assembly, but no one owned up. All the pupils thought it had been a good joke. Even those with hangovers.

I sit beside my friend, Velvet, in stalag three. It's

clear why her mum gave her that name; she has velvety brown eyes and skin as smooth as milky coffee. She could also chat for Great Britain. If there's ever a talking marathon, Velvet will win it. She even talks in her sleep. Mum really likes Velvet because she works hard at school and Mum thinks she's a good influence on me. I really like her because she's really nice.

Velvet did her talk a few days before me. Hers was on Indian cooking, and her mum made her some pakora to bring into school for us to try. Her mum makes the best pakora in the world – no – make that the universe.

When it was Velvet's turn to talk, she went out to the front of the class, gave everyone a big smile, and held up a round silvery tin with a close-fitting lid. She opened up the tin to reveal lots of little tins, each containing a different spice. Then she talked about all the different spices and what they were used for. I didn't know ginger was good for indigestion or that saffron came from the dried stigmas of the crocus. She finished off by handing round the pakora. Everyone said how good they were. Everyone that is, except Belinda Fishcake and her little gaggle of friends. The Beelines, we call them, for they always make a beeline for Belinda whenever she appears. They hang on her every word, always do what she wants to do and agree with everything she says. If Belinda came into school wearing a Donald Duck mask and told them to quack, they would. They haven't a brain cell among them. So when Belinda turned up her nose at the pakora, the Beelines did too. Velvet's happy smile vanished and even Mrs Jackson and I having extra helpings didn't help.

'Don't let Belinda and the Beelines get you down,' I said to Velvet later. 'They're not worth it.'

'I know,' said Velvet, and tried to cheer up. But I could tell she was still upset.

I wondered why the Beelines were like that. Why they couldn't think for themselves. Why they had to copy someone else's rotten behaviour. But I expect there are Beelines in every school. Like I said, I don't expect my school's much different from yours.

Of course I decided to talk about Grandma. Nothing else exciting had happened to me recently. I made notes of the interesting things Grandma talked about, like the huntsman spiders in Australia, big as soup plates, but harmless. Or the tiny redback spiders whose bite was deadly. Then there was the trunk of old clothes and all the things Grandma had done in the sixties. I read the notes out loud in bed and timed myself. I had much more than three minutes' worth, so I just kept in the really interesting stuff. No one would nod off while I was talking!

When my turn came to do my talk, though, I was really nervous. It seemed a long way out to the front of the class and my shoes developed a squeak they never had before. My knees felt wobbly and my throat dry, but I took a big deep breath and began . . .

'My grandma has a signed photograph of The Beatles. She went to see them in the Cavern in Liverpool before they were really famous . . .'

Everyone was interested, especially when I went on to talk about sixties' music and clothes and how the young people thought they were invincible. I didn't mean to say anything about Grandma being a model, because, of course, she hadn't been, but Belinda Fishcake started to yawn loudly and it was the only thing I could think of to say that would shut her up. It did. Her eyes opened wide in surprise and stayed like that till I'd finished.

'Well done, Abby,' said Mrs Jackson, 'and not too much over time. Your grandma sounds a very interesting lady. I'd like to meet her. I wonder if she would come and talk to the class and perhaps bring some of her vintage clothing with her?'

Out of the corner of my eye I could see Fishcake was furious.

'I'll ask Grandma and let you know,' I told Mrs Jackson.

I wasn't sure how she would feel about it.

She was delighted.

'I was a model once,' she grinned, 'during student charities' week in 1963. I only modelled hats, but we don't need to mention that!'

Mum, however, wasn't sure about all this at all.

'Are you certain you want to do this, Mum?' she said. 'Today's teenagers take no prisoners. If they don't like you they might shout rude things at you.'

Grandma grinned. 'Well I can shout rude things back, can't I? I know a few really good words.'

'No swearing,' squeaked Mum. 'And no telling tales of nearly getting expelled. Try to behave. I don't want to have to listen to complaints about *you* at parents' night as well.'

That was unfair. Setting fire to the Science lab had been an accident!

'I'll be as good as gold,' said Grandma. 'Come on, Abby. Help me sort through some of my stuff and tell me what you think your class would want to hear about.'

'Talk to them about music and fashion, Grandma. Nearly everyone's into that.'

'OK,' said Grandma. 'How about a fashion show with you as the model and some sixties' music in the background? I could show you how to dance the Twist and the Shake and everyone could join in.'

Brilliant! And educational too, of course!

But there was a problem. You can't play old records on a CD player, so the following Saturday Grandma and I trailed round the junk shops looking for an old record player. We finally ran a dark brown one to earth in a dingy little shop off the High Street. The shop owner wanted fifty pounds for it, but Grandma beat him down to twenty, which was all Mum had given us, and insisted that he clean it up for us. Underneath the dirt the record player was an eye-watering orange, except for the handle, which had once been genuine white plastic. We settled for dirty grey.

'I used to carry one like this round to my friend's house every Saturday night,' said Grandma, as we lugged it home. 'We danced the night away in her front room while her parents were at the cinema. Then her dad took me home at half-past ten.'

'I sometimes wonder what my dad is like,' I surprised myself by saying. I never mention him to Mum. It's not a subject she encourages.

Grandma put her arm round my shoulders and gave me a hug. 'Let's go and have an enormous ice cream and I'll tell you what I know.'

We found a quiet café off the main square and Grandma ordered the ice cream. They weren't exactly enormous so she ordered two more.

When we were finished Grandma sat back and said, 'What do you want to know about your dad?'

'Everything,' I said.

'Warts and all?'

'Warts and all.'

'Your mum was very young when she met him. He was a good-looking fellow – there's no doubt about that – older than your mum, but feckless.'

'Feckless?'

'Irresponsible.'

I made a mental note to add 'feckless' to my word collection.

'He couldn't keep a job and was for ever getting

into trouble. Your grandad and I didn't like him and tried to tell your mum he was no good. But she paid no heed. She upped and married him. The marriage didn't last and he left as soon as he knew you were on the way. Didn't want the responsibility, you see. Does that upset you?'

'No. Yes. I don't know,' I mumbled.

I had hoped there'd been another reason my dad had gone off. Like he'd lost his memory or something. Now I knew the truth.

Grandma let the silence between us grow for a while, then she went on, 'But your mum made up for him by being devoted to you, and working very hard to bring you up so well.'

'I know,' I said. 'But she's a bit much sometimes.'

Grandma laughed. 'I can see that. Perhaps we should do something about it. But first, let's just wow Mrs Jackson and your class at Cosgrove High.'

9

Over dinner a few nights later, Mum asked Grandma what she would wear to do her talk.

Grandma shrugged. 'Clothes, I suppose.'

Mum's lips tightened and she suggested she take Grandma out and buy her a sensible little suit for the occasion.

Grandma wasn't keen. 'I'm not the sensible little suit type. How about my jeans and my woolly sheep jumper?'

Mum shuddered. Grandma's jeans had washed out and up and the woolly sheep jumper had washed up and in. But they were Grandma.

'I think you should wear them,' I said. 'And old Belle and the crocodile boots. That's part of who you are, and you can tell the stories about them.'

Grandma beamed. 'Great, that's settled then.'

Mum opened her mouth to protest then closed it again quickly. She knew it was two against one.

Meantime, I was practising being a model. I threw back my shoulders, thrust out my hip bones and strode up and down my bedroom with a bored expression on my face. But my room's not very big and I kept bumping into furniture or falling over stuff I had left on the floor. I suppose I could have cleared it up. Nah. Too boring. I found another solution. Coming home from school one day I passed a rubbish skip. In among the bits of old carpet and plaster was a long plank. Just the thing to practise walking along. I hurried home to ask Grandma to give me a hand.

'No problem,' she said.

That's one of the things I like about Grandma. Positive thinking. Mum would have had a million reasons why she couldn't walk along the road carrying an old plank. Not Grandma.

Grandma and I manoeuvred the plank out of the skip. It wasn't easy and we got covered in plaster dust.

'Raiders of the Lost Skip,' I said, and began to hum the Indiana Jones theme tune. Grandma joined in, stopping only to say 'G'day' to people who looked at us as if we were mad.

One of these was Belinda Fishcake. We just *had* to meet her, didn't we?

'Going into the building business?' she sneered. 'Is your house falling down? I'm sure we've got some old wood in the garage you could have.'

Before I had a chance to reply, Grandma chipped in. 'That's very kind of you, my dear. Abby and I are thinking of building a shelter for diseased cats. It's such a pity that no one wants them when they're covered in runny sores and crusty scabs, isn't it? Perhaps you'd like to bring the wood over and help us? Better still, take one of the cats as a pet! That would be a real kindness. You'd like to help a smelly old diseased cat nobody wants, wouldn't you?'

Belinda paled. 'Yes, no, er well, I think I'm allergic.' And she hobbled away quickly on her new platform trainers.

I looked at Grandma in amazement. She was grinning all over her wrinkles.

'Building a shelter for diseased cats?' I squeaked.

'I said *thinking* about building a shelter for diseased cats,' said Grandma. 'We can always change our minds.'

Now I know why my mum's a lawyer. Being devious runs in the family.

Eventually we got home. Have you ever tried crossing a road or going round a corner with a large plank? It's not easy. We moved some of the sitting-room furniture and placed the plank diagonally across the carpet. I put on one of Grandma's mini dresses and practised walking along the plank: hips forward, nose in the air, bored expression. It worked well too, till I fell off and hit my knee on the coffee table. I was just giving it a rub when Mum came home. Did she enquire about the bump on my knee? She did not.

'Look at the dirt on the carpet,' she said. 'What have you two been up to now?'

I suppose we *should* have cleaned the plank before bringing it indoors, so Grandma and I carried it out into the garden and I practised there.

That wasn't easy either. The garden's not very big and the plank ended up under the washing line. I bet not many supermodels have their faces slapped with wet dish towels or suffer near strangulation by yellow plastic clothes lines.

Back indoors, Mum asked Grandma if she was going to practise her talk.

'No need to practise, Eva,' she said. 'I'll just tell it like it was.'

Mum ran her hands through her hair. 'That's what I'm afraid of,' she muttered.

10

Mrs Polanski's dog, Benson, had arrived. I came home from school to find him eating the inside of my old slippers. I didn't mind – the slippers were horrible, and he was welcome to them. Unfortunately, he'd also eaten a hole in the sofa cushion, and had obviously mistaken the leg of Mum's favourite chair for a bone.

'Oh no,' I cried. 'Bad dog, Benson.'

Benson wagged his tail and went on chewing the slippers. I put my rucksack down over the hole in the cushion and was just examining the chair leg when the front door banged and Mum was home.

'What are you doing home so early?' I yelped.

'Whatever happened to "Hello Mum, nice to see you. Glad you could get away from work at a reasonable time for a change"?'

'Er, yes, that as well,' I said, and tried to stand in front of Benson, the chewed slippers, cushion and chair leg, all at the same time. Mission impossible.

Even for a sumo wrestler on a chocolate binge. Anyway, Benson moved. What is it with dogs? Why do they immediately head for people who don't like them much? Why do they jump up and try to lick them like a giant lolly?

Mum got a fright, backed away from Benson, knocked my rucksack off the sofa, found the hole in the cushion, saw the leg of the chair and the chewed slippers, all at the same time.

You can imagine what she said, but just in case you can't it went sort of like . . .

'Whaaaat? Who . . . ? Get that miserable four-legged excuse for a dog out of here this minute. Just wait till I get hold of your grandmother! She is *history*!'

Mum didn't actually say that at all, but I'm not allowed to write rude words so that's the best I can do.

At that moment Grandma walked in. She took in the situation at a glance.

'Mrs Polanski's ticker went a bit dodgy in the night so she was taken into hospital sooner than expected. I had to go with her in the ambulance and they don't allow dogs. I'm sure she'll pay for any damage, though she is an old age pensioner, and doesn't have a lot. I'd said we'd look after the dog, so I couldn't let her down.'

Mum opened her mouth then shut it again with a snap. She snatched her foot away from Benson, who had tired of the slippers, and was now eating the little black leather tassels on her best black shoes.

'If you are responsible for this animal then kindly keep him under control and away from me. I shall be in my study.'

Mum's study is really just her bedroom with a desk in the corner, but I suppose study sounded better under the circumstances. She put on her best courtroom face and swept out of the room. It would have been a superb exit too, if she hadn't tripped over Benson and cracked her head on the edge of the door.

Grandma and I didn't dare laugh, though I could feel the laughter rumbling and tumbling inside me. But at least Benson looked impressed. He gave Mum such an adoring look and admiring wag of his tail that I'm sure he would have clapped his paws if he could.

When Mum's bedroom door clicked shut, Grandma sighed. 'Your mum really does need to lighten up, Abby,' she said. 'We *definitely* need to do something about it.'

The day of Grandma's talk arrived. Grandma was very calm. I was as nervous as a turkey at Christmas. Would I look all right in the dresses? Would I trip over the shiny boots and fall on my bum? Worst of all, would everybody laugh?

'Don't worry, you'll be right, Abby,' was all Grandma could say as she pulled on the crocodile boots and tramped out to the shed to rescue old Belle. Old Belle was none the worse for her visit to the spades and lawnmower, and still smelled to high heaven. Grandma greeted her like a long-lost friend and it may have been my over-active imagination, but I could have sworn the jacket baa-ed.

We piled the record player, records and a suitcase with the dresses in into the back of Mum's car and she dropped us off at school. Mrs Jackson was waiting for us at the front entrance.

'I've been looking out for you,' she said. 'You must be Abby's grandmother. I'm so glad to meet you. Abby's told us so much about you, and I'm sure your talk is going to be wonderful.' She stretched out her hand.

Grandma grinned and shook it. Mrs Jackson winced. Sometimes Grandma forgets she's not shearing sheep. Then Mrs Jackson's nostrils twitched.

'I think the wind's changed direction. We seem to be getting a whiff of the sewage works.'

'Terrible smell, sewage,' said Grandma, with a straight face, and followed Mrs Jackson inside.

Then came the bombshell. It was on the school notice board.

9.30 a.m. TALK BY MS APHRODITE HARRIS
IN SCHOOL HALL

I stopped dead and dropped the suitcase of clothes I was carrying on to Mrs Jackson's toe.

'Why are we in the school hall?' I yelped. 'Why aren't we in stalag three?'

Mrs Jackson removed the suitcase from her foot and explained . . .

'It's so good of your grandma to do this talk, Abby, that I invited all the classes in the year to attend. That's why I booked the school hall. It means we can use the platform to do the fashion parade. Isn't that splendid?'

My legs felt suddenly liquid. 'Great,' I said. 'Just great.'

Now I could make a fool of myself in front of a

hundred and fifty kids instead of just thirty.

But Grandma just looked at me and winked. She was enjoying herself.

It didn't take long to set things up. I had packed the clothes in the order that I would be wearing them, and Mrs Jackson had placed a screen that I could change behind in the corner of the stage. She'd also set up a table beside Grandma for the record player and the records.

'There now,' she said. 'Is there anything else that needs to be done before I bring the classes along?'

'Just give me a few minutes to put some make-up on Abby. We want to get the real sixties look.'

'Fine,' Mrs Jackson nodded. 'I'm really looking forward to this.' And she smiled and hurried away.

I got into the first outfit. It was a pale cream mini dress with a black hipster belt and long black shiny boots. Grandma applied some pale pancake make-up all over my face and lips then painted on some bright blue eye shadow and thick black eye liner. The final touch was two pairs of false eyelashes stuck on with adhesive. I'd never worn false eyelashes before and they made my eyelids feel very heavy. The eyelashes were so long they tickled my cheek, but they made me feel really glamorous. Then Grandma stuck on a few extra-long single lashes, and put some tiny black dots round the outside corners of my eyes. The only problem was my hair. There was no way it could be tamed into a Mary Quant sixties' bob, so we had to be content with tucking it up under a little black cap with a shiny peak.

I was ready for the world, but was the world ready for me? I peeped round from behind the screen. The school hall was filling up. Mrs Jackson was telling everyone to sit cross-legged on the floor. I hate sitting like that. It's extremely uncomfortable and makes your back ache. Though not Belinda Fishcake's apparently. Her voice carried over to me from the front row . . .

'I do this at yoga,' she was saying. 'It's very good for you. You sit like this and think of something beautiful and the beauty just shines through you.'

Baloney mahoney. She just likes to show off how long her legs are.

She was sitting right in the middle of the front row, surrounded by the Beelines. They were all practising their bored expressions. Well, I'd show them . . .

Mrs Jackson came to check that everything was ready and Grandma gave me the thumbs up sign as she left me behind the screen and went to sit at the table in the middle of the platform.

I could hear everyone gasp when they saw Grandma. She's not really like your average grandma, unless they all wear crocodile boots, faded old jeans and smelly sheepskin jackets.

Mrs Jackson had prepared a little introductory speech about how grateful she was to Grandma for coming along etc, and then it was Grandma's turn. She stood up, walked round the front of the table and looked at the audience.

'Gee, but that cross-legged thing looks bloody uncomfortable, and it'll most likely make you constipated. Why don't you all make yourselves comfortable, relax a bit and I'll tell you some stories.'

There was a little silence, then everybody giggled and unwound their legs. Grandma began . . .

'First off I want to introduce you to a friend of mine,' and she took off old Belle and told them her story.

Later she said . . .

'Now I want to introduce you to someone who *isn't* a friend of mine.' And she took off the crocodile boots. I could hear the gasp and I wondered if Grandma was wearing her favourite socks. She calls them her Sunday socks because they're holey.

Then she started to talk about what it was like being a young person in the sixties. She talked about the Vietnam War, flower power, hippies, the pill, and England winning the World Cup in 1966. That got a big cheer. But the great thing was she talked to her audience like they were sensible human beings. Why do some adults find that so difficult?

By this time I had started to relax. Things were going well. Grandma was doing fine. I heard her start to talk about music and fashion and I knew my fashion parade would start in a couple of minutes. I started to panic all over again. I closed my eyes and began to breathe deeply to calm the fluttering in my stomach. Then I heard Grandma say, 'And now my glamorous assistant, Abby, will model some of the sixties' fashions.'

She switched on the record player and The Beatles began to sing *Love, Love Me Do*. That was my cue to step out and model the first outfit. I took a last deep breath and opened my eyes. At least I tried to, but I couldn't. My eyelids were stuck together. Grandma must have put too much adhesive on the false eyelashes. I couldn't see out. I panicked, stepped forward, knocked over the screen, fell over my feet, and showed my knickers to the entire year.

Grandma shot to my aid calling . . .

'Time to get dancing, everyone! Go for it.' She upped the volume on the record player to ear-splitting, and while everyone scrambled to their feet and began dancing, she helped me up, and unstuck my eyelids.

'Damn stupid things,' she muttered. 'I should have remembered – they always did that to me too.'

My face was scarlet, but everyone else was too busy dancing to notice. I eventually did model all the clothes. I finished off by wearing Grandma's favourite, a flowery mini skirt, while everyone twisted to Lulu's *Shout*.

The entire year had a great time and didn't want to go back to 'normal' lessons.

'Wish we could have your grandma come and talk to us every day,' was what most people said to me later.

But Belinda Fishcake sneered . . .

'Only you could show your knickers to the school to get a laugh, Abigail Montgomery.'

I could have thumped her, but Velvet pulled me away, and giggled, 'At least they were new knickers, Abby.'

And they were. I'd bought them specially. Just in case.

12

Grandma and I came home full of what had happened at school. We talked and talked about it. Mum was pleased everything had gone well – I didn't mention my falling over – but didn't say too much. I felt a bit let down. I thought she would have been more enthusiastic. Then I thought, she's probably just tired. She's hoping to be made a partner in the firm and really does work hard. She brings a lot of work home, too; she's got more homework than I have. Not something to look forward to. When I leave school I want to be finished with homework.

By now it was obvious that Grandma and I got on so well, but things had started to get tricky with Mum. When she wasn't being quiet or busy, she was grumpy. Not ordinary 'Get your bedroom tidied this minute' grumpy, or that time of the month 'leave me alone I want to die' grumpy, but something else. Something I couldn't put my finger on. So I did the sensible thing. I asked her about it in plain simple terms.

'Why are you so grumpy, Mum?' I said.

I didn't get a plain simple answer. Instead I got a tirade (another of my words – it's what grown-ups do when they go on and on and on – you know the kind of thing, of course you do!).

'Why should I be grumpy? It's not as though I have all the housework to do myself.' (Not true. Grandma and I set the table once.) 'Or all the washing and ironing to do myself.' (I didn't point out that the washing machine does the washing and Grandma and I don't really care if our shirts aren't ironed.) 'All the hoovering and polishing to do myself.' (True. Grandma and I tried it, broke a crystal vase, and the Hoover blew up.) 'All the shopping to do myself.' (True. Grandma and I did that once too, but apparently we bought too many KitKats and beer, and not enough vegetables.) 'And I look after Benson.' (True. Mum hadn't exactly become a dog lover overnight, but Benson thought she was magic. He followed her everywhere. He sat by her chair. He wiggled his silky head under her hand so she would stroke him. He sat at the door expectantly as soon as he heard her car outside in the evening. He even slept by her bed. She put him outside her bedroom each night and closed the door, but by morning he was back. He offered her his undying devotion whether she wanted it or not. She said she didn't want it, though I reckoned she was weakening.

She'd recently started buying him doggy choc drops as a Saturday treat.)

'But you like Benson,' I said.

'That may be so.' She definitely was weakening. 'But he's just one more thing I have to attend to. While you and your grandma swan around having a wonderful time, I have to work to keep a roof over our heads. And you wonder why I'm grumpy!'

And she flounced out of the room, banging the sitting-room door behind her.

Grandma was in the kitchen making a beef stew, from some old Aboriginal recipe, she said, and had heard what was said.

She wiped her floury hands on the seat of her jeans. 'Fancy a walk to the ice cream shop, Abby?'

I didn't need to be asked twice. I put Benson on his lead and we exited quickly.

'Did you hear Mum going on and on, Grandma?' I said. 'It's not fair. We *do* try to help.'

'Hmm,' said Grandma. 'I wonder.'

I didn't have time to ask Grandma what she wondered because Benson got the scent of another dog and practically jerked me off my feet as he pulled me faster and faster down the road. He only stopped when we got to the ice cream shop where his pal, a Jack Russell terrier imaginatively called Jack, was tied up outside. Jack's owner was a boy called Andy Gray, a year ahead of me in school.

Andy came out of the shop with two cones, one

for himself and one for Jack. He saw me with Benson.

'Hi, Knobbly Knees!' He'd heard about the mini dress fashion show, then.

'Hi, Banana Feet,' I said. He already had policeman-sized feet.

We grinned. We actually quite liked each other, but of course, would *never* say so.

'Got much homework?' Andy asked.

'Loads,' I said.

'Me too,' he nodded, and went off with Jack.

Wow, I thought, he *definitely* likes me. That was nearly a whole conversation. I would go over the entire episode later in my head and count the words.

Grandma caught up with me, searched in the pocket of her jeans and found no money. A common occurrence. Fortunately I still had some pocket money left, but only enough for one cone, so we took turns licking it on the way back. I broke off the bottom bit, put some ice cream on it and gave it to Benson.

'You spoil that dog,' said Grandma.

'Not as much as Mum,' I said. 'He gets more chocolate than I do.'

Grandma nodded. 'He gives your mum a lot of love and affection.'

'So do I,' I said, slightly miffed. 'It's always been just the two of us.'

'Till I came along,' said Grandma. 'Now there's three and I think that's partly why your mum's so grumpy. I don't think she likes sharing you. You and I get along real well, don't we?'

I nodded. It was true. Grandma was more like someone my age. I don't know exactly how old she was in years, but that didn't seem to matter. Somehow I had the feeling that Mum had been born old. I said as much to Grandma.

'No, that's not fair,' she said. 'Your mum's just had to be very responsible all the time, and now I think she's feeling a bit left out. I think that's one reason why she's so grumpy.'

I thought about that while we licked the ice cream. Grandma had a point. I'd have to be a bit nicer to Mum. Pour soul, perhaps she felt nobody loved her.

'Is there another reason why she's so grumpy, then?' I asked.

'She needs a man,' said Grandma.

I nearly choked on the ice cream. Grandma obligingly thumped me on the back while Benson looked sympathetic. When I'd stopped coughing and my eyes had stopped streaming, I thought again about how Grandma treated me like an intelligent human being. And, as an intelligent, i.e. nosey, human being, I needed to hear more.

'I think Benson needs a bit more exercise, Grandma,' I said. 'We'll go home the long way round. Now what was that you were saying about Mum needing a man?'

13

Grandma explained that she thought Mum needed a bit of fun in her life.

'She needs someone to take her out,' she said. 'For dinner, or to the cinema, or even just for a walk in the park. She needs to be herself sometimes, not my daughter or your mother or the breadwinner, housekeeper, whatever.'

I had to think about that for a moment. It was something I hadn't considered before. Thing is, your mum's your mum, isn't she? You never actually think of her as a person. Someone who might want to stay up late or not go to work, or buy new clothes instead of a new Hoover.

'But where would she meet someone to take her out?' I said. 'She never goes anywhere except work, and I've seen some of the men there. They're ancient.'

'We'll try to encourage her to go out a bit more. If she won't go on her own, we could go with her, and if we see someone suitable, try to give her a push in his direction.'

I was dubious. 'It's not much of a plan, Grandma. It's a bit vague, and Mum's bound to be suspicious. She's a lawyer after all. She's paid to be suspicious.'

'I know,' said Grandma, 'but it's the best I can come up with at the moment. Let's call it Operation Boyfriend. So keep your eyes peeled for any likely men, and remember to keep it a secret from your mum.'

Easier said than done.

So was looking for a suitable man. The only place I met any men was in school. And they weren't real men, they were teachers. Then I thought about Mum being a person and not just a mum and I tried to think about teachers being people and not just teachers. Very difficult. I had a word with Velvet about it. Velvet's very good at solving problems, especially in Maths. She has a very logical mind. Unlike me.

We were sitting in the dinner hall having our packed lunches and had just swapped a tuna fish roll (mine) for an onion bhaji (hers), when I told her about the problem. Velvet bit thoughtfully into the tuna fish roll.

'Let's start off with the teachers you like,' she said. 'No point in getting your mum a date with someone you can't stand.'

Little Miss Logic, like I said.

We sat and made a list as we munched.

My favourite teacher is Mr Morrison. He takes us for History. He's got twinkly eyes, and a crooked smile. He always makes History come alive and is so interesting we hang on his every word. Of course, he's nice to look at as well.

But Velvet shook her head.

'He's everybody's favourite,' she said. 'But he's got a wife and three kids, so he's out.'

Hmm, pity.

'There's Mad Max,' I said.

He takes us for Art. He's really scruffy and always covered in paint, but he doesn't mind us chatting so long as we keep working. He said my abstract design was quite good last week.

Again Velvet shook her head.

'He's keen on Miss McKenzie. They're always waiting behind at break to chat to each other, and Danny Plover in Three B says he saw them snogging in the car park. But he may have made that up, though Mad Max does give her a lift sometimes in his old Beetle.'

'What about Mr Powers, the French teacher? I quite like him.'

'Nope,' said Velvet, through a mouthful of samosa. 'He lives with his mum, who's an invalid, and anyway, Ms Oldroyd the German teacher's been after him for ages.'

I looked at her in amazement. 'How come you know so much about everybody?'

'They all come into the shop,' said Velvet. 'I just keep my head down and my ears open.'

Of course! I'd forgotten about the shop. Velvet's

mum and dad have the little post office cum grocer's near the school. Everyone goes in there for their odds and ends. Velvet's mum knows who's on a diet, who's given up smoking, who's thinking of buying a new car, just by the things they buy or stop buying.

'Who does that leave then? I don't know any of the others very well.'

'We'll ask Mum after school,' said Velvet. 'She'll know who's available.'

Mrs Guha was folding up the evening papers for Velvet's paper round when we got to the shop.

'Hullo, Abby,' she greeted me. 'How are you? You hungry? Fresh pakora in the back shop. You go eat.'

'Thank you, Mrs Guha, I'll go in a minute, but first . . .'

I swore her to secrecy, then told her the problem.

Mrs Guha frowned and shook her head.

'There's no one really suitable I can think of at the moment. Mr Soames . . .'

'Our Maths teacher.' I made a face.

'. . . his wife's just had a baby and he's not getting much sleep. He's really grumpy in the morning. Mr Burnett is saving up for a new car and can't afford to go out at night, and Mr Springfield's long-term girlfriend is coming home next week from her year away in Canada. All the others are too old and too deadery.'

Deadery?

'*Doddery*, Mum,' grinned Velvet.

'But I tell you what,' Mrs Guha brightened up. 'We could look for a nice Indian doctor for your mum. Or maybe a pharmacist. My cousin's husband's brother is coming to this country, maybe we could arrange something.'

'All right, Mum, calm down! Don't you go matchmaking,' laughed Velvet. 'And don't tell anyone – this is supposed to be a secret.'

'Oh yes yes,' said Mrs Guha. 'A secret. Of course. I am very good with secrets.'

By the time I got home Mum had phoned to say she had to work late again, so Grandma and I ate on our own. We gave the veggie burgers a body swerve and had sausage, egg and chips. It was great. I like my egg really runny so I can dip my chips into the yolk. It was during this dipping delight that I filled Grandma in on the lack of progress on the man hunt.

Grandma speared a chip and nibbled off the end.

'We've got to come up with something. I think deep down your mum's quite lonely.'

'Lonely!' I cried and jumped up, sending my last sausage hurtling to the floor. 'There's a lonely hearts column in the evening newspaper! Let's have a look at that.'

I found the evening paper, turned to the personal

ads page and propped it up with the tomato-sauce bottle.

'What a lot of lonely people there are,' I said, looking at the long columns. 'How do we choose?'

'Well,' said Grandma, pointing to one ad. 'Sometimes people reveal more than they intend to in these things. What do you think of someone who describes himself as "tall, dark, handsome and every woman's dream"?'

'Plonker,' I said. 'Probably every woman's nightmare.'

'Right,' said Grandma. 'Put a line through that one. What about "Big Cuddly Bear looking for Little Cuddly Bear"?'

'Idiot. Should try the zoo.'

We were just putting a line through 'Male, own house and car seeks similar female' – stingy, we reckoned, when Mum came home and caught us.

'What are you two up to?' she said, as we gave a guilty start.

'Nothing,' we said.

Mum gave us her 'I know you are lying through your teeth' look, and picked up the paper.

'Lonely hearts,' she said. 'You're surely not thinking of getting married again, Mum?'

Grandma and I looked at each other.

'Oh, just looking,' said Grandma.

'Well, really,' sniffed Mum. 'Handsome Harris is hardly cold, and already you're looking for another man. I think that's disgraceful.'

Grandma tried to look suitably ashamed. Her shoulders drooped, her mouth drooped and she gave a deep sigh. In fact, she could have fooled me, if it hadn't been for the slow wink. 'Well, if you're lonely, Eva . . .' she said.

'How can you possibly be lonely?' said Mum. 'Living with your daughter, granddaughter, a demented dog, and the remains of the Australian outback in the cupboard?'

Grandma sighed again. 'You can be lonely in the middle of a crowd of people, Eva. You should know that.'

Mum said nothing, just strode into the kitchen and began cooking her own dinner. But, judging by the amount of blue smoke that drifted out into the hallway, she was taking her annoyance out on the veggie burgers.

14

I am hopping, fizzing, steam coming out of every pore mad. Mad mad mad. With Belinda Fishcake.

After meeting Andy and Jack the other night, I met Andy on the bus going to school as well. I'd just caught the bus by the skin of my teeth, or my shins actually, as I fell up the step on to the platform. I struggled to my feet and a voice said, 'You all right, Abby?'

Four more words from Andy. Added to the eight from our last conversation this was a record. We were practically engaged!

I mumbled something inaudible, aware that my face had gone as pink as a baboon's backside. Then I looked up and had to decide where to sit. There were two choices: further up the bus beside Belinda Fishcake, or in the empty seat beside Andy. There was no contest.

'Are you sure you're all right?' Andy asked again. 'That looks like a nasty scrape you've got.'

'Oh it's nothing,' I said, airily. Actually it stung

like the devil. I made a mental note to scream later.

'So why are you on this bus?' I asked. 'You're not usually. Not that you haven't a perfect right to go on any bus you want. I mean, it's a free country. Not that the buses are free. Unless you're a pensioner which you're not, obviously.'

I was burbling like an idiot. Shut up, Abby, I told myself. SHUT UP!

I took my own advice and closed my mouth so quickly I bit my tongue. That brought tears to my eyes. Have you ever tried to reabsorb two eyelidsful of tears while silently screaming through your ears? It's tricky.

Fortunately Andy didn't seem to notice.

'My gran's not very well,' he said, 'so I stayed with her last night to walk her dog. He's a large German shepherd with no sense at all. He was chasing rabbits on the common this morning wondering why they wouldn't stay to play with him.'

'Benson's not much better,' I told him, and we happily swapped dog stories for the rest of the journey. We would probably have got off the bus and walked into school together if Belinda Fishcake hadn't spotted us. When it got to our stop, she stood up and came up the bus towards us. Her perfectly arched eyebrows lifted in surprise when she saw us. Then, when the bus gave a little jolt as it slowed, she pretended to stumble and practically threw herself on to Andy's lap. Naturally he put out a hand to help her.

'Oh, thank you, Andy,' she said in her very best little girl lost voice. 'I'm so glad you were there to save me.'

YUK YUK YUK VOMIT VOMIT VOMIT.

And she held on to his hand like it was the last life belt on the *Titanic*.

'Oh dear,' she said, and I swear her bottom lip trembled. 'Oh dear, I think I may have twisted my ankle. Could you possibly help me into school, Andy?'

'Sure,' said Andy. 'Take my arm and lean on me. Abby will carry your rucksack, won't you, Abby?'

I nodded. Speechless. Stony-faced.

Belinda smiled at me triumphantly, and I was sorely tempted to kick her other ankle. As it was, I had to carry her rucksack into school.

The Beelines made a beeline for Belinda when they saw her.

'What happened, Belinda?' they fussed. 'Are you all right?'

'Oh, it's nothing,' said Belinda, giving a little pretend wince of pain. 'And Andy's just been so good.'

Andy smiled and handed her over to her friends.

'Take care of that ankle now,' he said, and without even a glance at me, wandered away.

I dropped Belinda's rucksack on to her toe, just so she'd know I wasn't fooled for one minute, and she laughed; that little, silvery, tinkly laugh that makes you want to spit.

'Better luck next time, Scabigail,' she called out.

Did you hear what she called me! SCABIGAIL! I'll fix her one of these days. I'll get my own back, just see if I don't.

I'm mad mad mad. With Belinda Fishcake. But I may have mentioned that.

15

After a few days, Mrs Polanski got out of hospital, though she was still very weak. Grandma and I took Benson round to visit her. Benson wagged his tail and Mrs Polanski stroked his silky head.

'I hope you've been a good boy, Benson,' she said, 'and not given any trouble.'

Benson gave her his hurt 'As if I would' look, and Mrs Polanski laughed.

'He knows everything you say, that dog. He just doesn't do anything about it.'

Benson wandered off to sniff around, and Mrs Polanski motioned us over to her chair so she could whisper. 'I don't want Benson to hear,' she said.

We leaned close.

'It's about Benson. I really can't look after him any more, but I couldn't possibly send him to the V-E-T to be P-U-T D-O-W-N,' she spelled. 'All my other friends are as old as I am and can't look after him either. You are my only young friends. Do you think you could have Benson permanently?'

'Oh yes,' I said, and looked at Grandma.

'No worries,' she said, and looked at me.

We both knew the only problem would be Mum, but we'd get round that. Somehow.

'Good.' Mrs Polanski relaxed back into her chair. 'I'm so glad that's settled. It's a weight off my mind. I've been worrying about it ever since I went into hospital with that little heart scare. Then there's my bunions. I don't know when they'll get done now. The only other thing is, could I possibly come and visit Benson sometimes? Perhaps when I'm feeling a bit lonely?'

'Of course,' we said. 'No problem.'

Or so we thought.

It turned out that Mrs Polanski had lots of pensioner friends who were very fond of Benson, and once Mrs Polanski was up and around they all came to visit him. I heard the noise as I came along the road from school a few days later. The sitting-room windows were open and there was the sound of a mouth organ playing and crackly voices singing,

'Daisy, Daisy, give me your answer do.

I'm half crazy, oh for the love of you . . .' or something like that.

It was cheerful if not tuneful.

I opened the front door and immediately fell over a zimmer frame. Grandma appeared in the hall carrying a large tray full of mugs of tea and cream buns.

'This is their third lot of tea,' she said. 'They just can't stop singing.'

'And dancing,' I said, as I opened the sitting-room door and saw two old ladies waltzing up and down the sitting-room carpet.

An elderly gentleman with wispy grey hair and a mouth organ was sitting in Mum's favourite chair, playing his socks off.

Daisy, Daisy gave way to an Irish jig and there was much wheeching and hooching and tapping of feet and walking sticks. Grandma couldn't resist joining in and jigged her way across the sitting room with the tea tray. It was a pity that Mrs Polanski dropped her walking stick just then. It was a pity Grandma fell over it. It was a pity the tray, the tea and the cream buns went everywhere. It was a *great* pity Mum chose that day to leave the office early and bring work home. She walked in, just at the wrong moment.

Everyone froze, and looked guiltily at Mum. Her expression would have curdled the cream in the buns.

'Mother,' she said. 'I would like to speak to you in my study.'

Oh-oh. Telling off time.

It was worse than that. Grandma really caught it. It started off with 'That dog brings nothing but trouble.' Then, 'Irresponsible' was the word most often used, closely followed by 'Bad example', hotly pursued by 'Totally disruptive', with 'Menace to society' bringing up the rear.

I thought that was a bit much.

In between picking up the bits of mug we could hear Grandma protesting that it was only a little tea party and wasn't Mum going a bit over the top?

'*Over the top!*' screeched Mum.

Silently we cleared away as best we could. Benson helped by gorging on the cream buns and licking up any stray splashes from the upholstery. Mrs Polanski and the pensioners slipped away quietly, and, by the time Mum and Grandma came back downstairs, order had been restored.

'See, Eva,' beamed Grandma. 'Nothing to fuss about. Everything is cleared away. It's all neat and tidy.'

And with perfect timing and a great harumph Benson chose that precise moment to throw up on the sitting-room carpet.

16

Life was a little quieter for a few weeks after that. To keep the peace, I was on my best behaviour. So were Grandma and Benson. He was also on a strict diet, only getting to eat what was good for him. No human food. Certainly no cream buns. Benson hated it. He checked out the dried pellets in his dish every day and slumped to the floor in disgust. He'd have phoned the RSPCA if he could. But that wasn't all.

'Now that, owing to some very irresponsible people in this house, Benson is officially ours,' intoned Mum, 'he will have to be looked after properly, walked regularly, and deloused before he even looks like he needs it. Furthermore,' (she really does sound like a lawyer sometimes) 'he will have to be properly trained. Abby, you will take him to dog-training classes.'

I clicked my heels and gave a Nazi salute. Mum ignored me. Grandma muttered 'Strewth,' and Benson sank to the floor in disbelief.

'Dog-training classes,' I muttered, when Mum had left the room. 'Benson's too old for dog-training classes. The class will be full of puppies weeing everywhere and chasing their tails. Benson's going to feel out of it. He's going to be psychologically damaged.'

I hope I spelled psychologically right. It's one of my new words. I use it whenever I can to impress people.

'Look on the bright side,' said Grandma. 'You might see someone there suitable for you know who.' And she pointed in the direction of the kitchen.

'Of course,' I said. 'That's a possibility, but first I'll have to find out where the classes are held.'

I asked Velvet.

'Mum will know about dog-training classes,' she said. 'Come to the shop after school.'

We didn't have to ask about the classes, there was a postcard in the shop window advertising them, every Wednesday evening, in the scout hall.

'I would come with you,' laughed Velvet, 'but I've only got a parrot.'

I went along the following Wednesday with Benson. The scout hall was a twenty-minute walk away from our house. I suggested to Mum that she might like to give Benson and me a lift, but she went into her 'I am not a chauffeur' and 'Your feet are designed for walking' and 'I do not want dog hairs all over my car' routine. So we walked. At least I walked. Benson dodged this way and that, zigzagging across the pavement, sneaking up every alleyway; so that by the time we got to the scout hall, he had smelled every smell in the entire universe and was totally exhausted.

The scout hall smelled of damp and old gym shoes. As soon as the dog trainer, a stern-looking lady in a tweed suit, said 'Get your dog to sit at heel,' Benson lay down and went to sleep.

'Benson,' I hissed. 'Benson, wake up.' Benson snored loudly.

The lady trainer was not amused, but someone else was.

'Nice one, Abby,' said a familiar voice behind me.

'Andy!' I turned round. 'What are you doing here?'

Silly question, he was holding on to his gran's daft German shepherd.

'Trying to get Humphrey better trained so he's easier for Gran to manage.'

'Any luck?' I asked.

'Dog doesn't understand English,' he said.

'Try German,' I grinned.

Andy grinned back and I completely forgot I was supposed to be training Benson and looking out for a suitable man for Mum.

17

The trouble with being on your best behaviour is that nobody notices. They notice when you behave badly, like being out late or being cheeky to a teacher, but when you're being Miss Goody Two-Shoes nobody notices at all.

Did Mum say, 'Well done, Abby,' when I tidied my room and put out three black sackfuls of rubbish? She did not. Did she say, 'Well done, Abby,' when I brushed Benson's coat till it gleamed so much he looked like someone else's dog? She did not. Did she say, 'Well done, Abby,' when I made a delicious meal of beans on toast for her when she came home really late from work one night? She did not. So, I gave it up. What's the point of being good if nobody notices, and it doesn't make any difference? Which it didn't. Mum was still grumpy, or cranky, as Grandma said one day . . .

'You're so cranky, Eva. If it's not your hormones, maybe it's your diet. I read somewhere that your diet can affect your mood.'

'There is nothing wrong with my diet,' said Mum. 'It is a perfectly healthy diet.'

'Yeah, but it looks disgusting,' said Grandma. 'Or maybe it's just the way you cook it. And all these vitamin pills. All they do is make you rattle. You'd be better off with a big juicy steak.'

That did it. Grandma had obviously given up on good behaviour too.

Mum's face went the unattractive shade of dried-up chewing gum.

'I will eat what I want to eat. Need I remind you this is *my* house. You do not contribute anything to it financially, so I will buy what food I like, and I would be obliged if you would keep your opinions about my diet to yourself.'

Oops. Time to exit stage left. I headed for the door. So did Benson, closely followed by Grandma. We wandered into town, then down through the precinct. It was empty at that time of night apart from an empty Coke can rattling in the breeze.

At first Grandma was quiet, not like her at all. Then she said, 'Maybe I shouldn't have come back, Abby. Maybe that was a mistake. I never was any good at keeping my big mouth shut. Maybe I should have stayed in Australia.'

I frowned. That was a lot of maybes from Grandma. She was usually so sure of things.

'Maybe you should stop being so silly,' I said. 'I'm really glad you're here.'

She gave me a quick hug.

'Not so sure about your mum, though. She's right about me not putting any money into the house.'

'But you cheer us all up, and you got us Benson, and my class think you're magic. That's worth more than money.'

Grandma hugged me again and grinned. Then, as we passed the supermarket, her grin widened. 'Hey now, look at that notice. Maybe I can do something about the money as well.'

18

'You've got a job *where?*' screeched Mum next day.

'In the supermarket,' said Grandma. 'Stacking shelves. Starting this evening, so I'll still be able to look after Benson during the day, and I can put some money into the household budget.'

'My mother, stacking supermarket shelves,' muttered Mum. 'What will the people at work think? I'm hoping to be made a partner in the firm and you get a job stacking shelves. Are you deliberately trying to show me up?'

'No,' said Grandma. 'I've got an honest job which will earn me some money. I'm not doing anything to you. You're just being a bit of a snob, that's all.'

Mum opened her mouth then shut it again. It was shut through most of dinner, only opening for the cheese omelette and salad to go in. Then Grandma left for work and we could hear her singing 'Hi ho hi ho, it's off to work we go' as she went down the path, calling a cheery 'Hullo' to the neighbours across the street and telling them she was off to her new job.

Mum closed her eyes and sighed. Then she looked at me. 'I told you your grandmother was untidy, airy-fairy, selfish and disruptive, didn't I?'

I nodded.

'Then add stubborn, pig-headed, and downright outrageous to that as well,' muttered Mum.

'But good fun too,' I added foolishly.

'Oh, I should have known you'd be on her side,' said Mum. 'She swans in here, upsets everything, and you think it's great. Well, thanks for the loyalty, Abby.'

Oh-oh, this was getting heavy.

I did my usual shrug, which is the best I can do when I can't think of a better answer, and that annoyed Mum even more, so I beat a hasty retreat to my bedroom and left Mum sitting on the sofa with only Benson for company.

I lay in bed that night and had a worry. I knew I was having a worry when I bit so far down a thumbnail that it hurt.

I loved Grandma and I loved Mum. But they were very different people, and though I was sure they loved each other, they were finding it very hard to live together. I was finding it hard to live with both of them, too. More and more, I was becoming Abby in the middle.

19

Grandma's job in the supermarket only lasted a week. She didn't like how the shelves were arranged so she rearranged them to let the old people get their shopping more easily. She put the sugar beside the tea and the bread beside the butter. She put out chairs so that folks coming in after work could have a rest, and she soothed crying babies while their mums went round with their trolleys. She told the manager she was making the shop more people-friendly. The manager wasn't impressed.

'The shop is here to make money,' he said. '*You* are making nothing but trouble. Please leave.'

After that, Grandma seriously thought about leaving us too.

'But you can't go,' I said, as I found her in her room one day with her big trunk in the middle of the floor, and old Belle and the crocodile boots on a chair. 'I like having you here. I want you to stay. Who'll look after Benson during the day if you go? Who'll get Mrs Polanski's shopping, and what about

Operation Boyfriend? Have you forgotten about that? You can't just swan off and abandon our secret project!'

Help, I was starting to sound like Mum!

'I know. I know,' sighed Grandma. 'But we haven't been very successful at finding any suitable men, have we? The only thing I've been successful at doing is annoying your mum.'

And she blew her nose loudly on a handkerchief with a picture of a kangaroo in the corner.

'I remember you sent me some hankies like that,' I said.

'I've got some more of them in my trunk,' said Grandma. She poked among the contents and came up with – not Australian wildlife hankies, but a little black book.

'Oh gee,' said Grandma. 'My little black book. I'd forgotten about that.'

'What is it?' I asked. 'An address book?'

'And then some,' smiled Grandma. 'In here are the names and addresses of all my old boyfriends.'

'Wow,' I said, impressed. 'There are *loads* of them!'

'They weren't all serious boyfriends. Some of them were friends who just happened to be boys. There's a difference.'

She sat back on her heels and began to go through the book.

'Oh,' she said. 'Malcolm McConnell. I haven't thought about him in years. Terrible rogue. Always in trouble. Nice chap. I really liked him. And Eddie

Phillips. Very musical. Played the double bass in an orchestra. But he had terrible acne, made him very shy. Jasper Robertson. Now he was a clever fellow. Great sense of humour. We went to a hippy festival together in the sixties. We painted our faces, wore flowers in our hair and didn't wash much. Those were the days!'

Grandma reminisced some more before closing the book. She was just putting it back into the trunk when . . .

'I've got it!' she yelled.

'What?' I asked, when she didn't go on. 'Yellow fever? The plague? A boil on your bum? All of the aforementioned?'

Grandma grinned. 'Better than that. I've got the answer to our secret project. A man for your mum.'

I looked at Grandma sceptically (that's another of my words. Officially it means doubtfully. Here it means I thought she was several kangaroos short of a mob).

'No offence, Grandma,' I said. 'But the men in your little black book are all going to be your age. I was picturing someone a bit younger for Mum.'

'I'm not talking about these men,' laughed Grandma. 'I'm talking about their offspring. Some of my old boyfriends are bound to have sons. We could track them down and find out.'

I looked at Grandma. Only she could have come up with such a hairbrained scheme. But it was so off the wall, it might just work . . .

77

20

Despite Grandma's best efforts, she was only able to trace three old boyfriends from her list. The others had left no forwarding address or had moved too far away.

'It's not many,' said Grandma, 'but it'll have to do. Who shall we begin with?'

I looked at the names. Malcolm McConnell. Colin Birkmyre. Charles Anderson.

'Let's start with Malcolm McConnell,' I said. 'You said you liked him.'

'I did,' said Grandma. 'He was very good-looking. Lots of thick black hair and a cheeky grin. But I suppose he'll have changed a bit by now. We'll try phoning him first.'

Grandma got his number from directory enquiries and dialled.

'Hullo,' said a man's voice.

'Hullo,' said Grandma. 'Malcolm?'

'Who is this?' said the voice.

'It's Aphrodite. We met in Liverpool in the sixties.

Do you remember?'

There was a pause.

'Malcolm's not here at the moment.'

'Well, I'd like to see him,' said Grandma. 'Can I come over? When will he be around?'

'Come on Saturday at two-fifteen,' said the voice.

'OK,' said Grandma, as the phone went dead.

'Strange man,' shrugged Grandma. 'But then Malcolm always did have some strange friends.'

'I wouldn't call you *that* strange, Grandma,' I grinned. 'Just mildly eccentric.'

'Only mildly? I was hoping for extremely. I can see I'll have to do better. What would you call extremely eccentric in a woman of my age?'

I thought, but not for long.

'Eating a sherbet dip while walking along the High Street. With her granddaughter eating the same, of course.'

'OK,' said Grandma. 'Let's take Benson to the café and buy the sherbet dips. I do have a reputation to work on.'

The following Saturday, the tricky thing was not telling Mum where we were going. I had been helping her with the shopping on Saturday afternoons in an effort to keep the peace, and she was expecting me to go with her as usual. Unfortunately she had planned to take me to the coffee shop in the High Street that afternoon as a treat. I felt rotten letting her down.

'Erm, all right if I don't come with you today, Mum?' I said. 'I promised Grandma I'd go with her to look up an old friend.'

It seemed best to stick as close to the truth as possible – less chance of being caught out.

'Oh.' Mum looked very let down, then rather suspicious. 'I haven't heard her mention any old friend. Whereabouts does this old friend live?'

'Not sure,' I said vaguely. 'About a couple of train stops away, I think. We'll take Benson with us so you don't need to worry about him, and we'll be back in time for tea.'

'All right,' said Mum. 'But I'm relying on you, Abigail, to keep your grandmother out of trouble.'

'There'll be no trouble. It's only a visit to an old friend.'

I should have known better.

The weather had turned cooler, so Grandma decided to wear old Belle and the crocodile boots for the trip. We got some very odd looks as we stood on the platform waiting for the train. Grandma didn't mind. If anyone stared too hard she simply said 'G'day, mate,' and they looked away quickly. They *moved* away quickly too when they got a whiff of old Belle. I'd got used to the smell by now, though Benson was still suspicious and growled every so often just to let old Belle know he was there. Still, it meant we had plenty of room on the train. No one came near us.

Grandma looked out of the window and admired the countryside.

'I'd forgotten how green everything is,' she said. 'The sheep farm was very dry and dusty. It was a hard life for a woman, living in the middle of nowhere, but Handsome Harris made it all worth while. He's a lovely man.'

'Was, Grandma,' I said gently.

'Yes, of course,' said Grandma. 'Was.'

She talked about how she'd met Handsome Harris. How she'd gone to the Gold Coast in Australia to visit an old school friend who had settled there, and had met Handsome Harris at Surfer's Paradise.

'Norma and I had just sat down outside a little café to have a cold beer and watch the surfers walk by when this fellow comes over and asks if he can buy us a drink. He was new in town and didn't know anybody. He was on holiday too and very charming. We talked for ages then parted company. I thought no more of it till he turned up at Norma's place two days later and asked me out for dinner. Apparently it had taken him two days to pluck up the courage. And that was that. We got on famously. He was a lovely man. Not very good with money, but a lovely man. I miss him.'

A little silence fell as the train slid into our station. Then Grandma gathered herself together and said, 'Now we have to find another lovely man for your mum. Come on, Benson, giddy up there.'

Grandma asked a man at the information desk directions to 6, Caldwell Street, and, after a suspicious sniff and a muttered 'Bloomin' gasworks' he told us how to get there.

It was only a short walk from the station, through a few streets of run-down red brick houses. Some of the houses were empty and boarded up. Most grew beer cans instead of flowers in their gardens.

I looked round, glad of Grandma and Benson's company. 'I don't like this place much,' I said.

'No,' sighed Grandma. 'Looks like Malcolm hasn't done very well for himself. Well, we're here now so we might as well carry on. You never know what will turn up.'

The police. That's what turned up!

Number 6 Caldwell Street was much the same as the rest of the houses in the street. It had a front door with blue peeling paint and a rusty door knocker. Grandma lifted up the knocker and it came away in her hand.

'Strewth,' she muttered, and dropped it in the garden.

She rapped her knuckles hard on the door. It swung open slowly, revealing a hallway with dirty grey walls and a matching carpet. Grandma pushed the door open wider.

'Malcolm,' she called. 'Are you there? It's Aphrodite.' She stepped inside.

That's when the men in the grey suits got her.

Benson yelped, but they ignored him. I yelped,

but they ignored me. Grandma dug a crocodile-boot heel into a big toe, a bony elbow into a groin, and was going for a nose with a killer tweak when the grey suits yelled, 'Police!'

Grandma stared them down. 'Prove it,' she said.

The warrant cards looked real. So did the police car that slid round the corner.

'What's all this about?' demanded Grandma. 'Has this country changed so much in the past few years that you can't come to visit an old friend without being set upon by the police?'

'The old friend is what this is all about,' said the eldest of the grey suits. 'Now if you've quite finished duffing us up, madam, we'll discuss it down at the station.'

Through it all I thought, 'Duffing us up.' Good little phrase. Must add that to my collection.

21

I told you that Mrs Jackson, my English teacher, said I have an over-active imagination? Well now it went into overdrive.

Had we been arrested, and if so, why . . . ?

Possibility 1
Grandma Aphrodite wasn't really my grandma, but a spy masquerading (appearing in disguise – one of my latest words) as a blood relative. She was so good she had fooled my mum and me and Benson – though he'd always been suspicious of old Belle.

Trouble was, in all the old spy movies I'd ever seen, the baddie had never ever had an Australian accent. It just wasn't threatening enough somehow.

Possibility 2
Malcolm McConnell had just been murdered by a blow to the head with a frozen leg of lamb – a friend of old Belle's possibly – and was lying behind the door, just out of sight. The police had arrived

to investigate and Grandma and I, and possibly Benson, were suspects.

Trouble was, there was no forensic team. In all the good cop shows I'd ever seen, there was always a forensic team, in white overalls, at a murder scene.

Possibility 3
The policemen were really dog catchers in disguise and were after Benson for some evil experiments to do with world domination – I hadn't quite worked out the details on this one yet.

Trouble was, there was a really nice WPC in the back of the police car with us who was chatting to Benson, telling him what a good boy he was, and that she had a dog at home just like him. She stroked Benson's silky ears and he loved it. Traitor!

At the police station, Grandma, never one to go quietly, was demanding her rights which included our immediate release, a telephone, a lawyer, a cup of tea with plenty of milk (no sugar), Coke for me, water for Benson, and a grovelling apology for considerable inconvenience caused to us, the entirely innocent, tax-paying public.

I got the Coke. Benson got the water. Grandma got led away to an interview room. The WPC sat with Benson and me and chatted. I was suspicious. Was she part of the good cop, bad cop game? Would the bad cop suddenly appear and yell at us? Was she trying to soften us up with the Coke? Was it truth-drugged? Was she psychologically (I knew that word would come in handy) trained to know my innermost thoughts? Well, if she was, she was really clever because, as far as I could see, she was just telling me not to worry, that Grandma would be back shortly, and asking me if I'd like a biscuit to go with my Coke. At the mention of the magic word 'biscuit' Benson wagged his tail and nuzzled her hand. That dog would make a rotten spy. He'd give away all your secrets for a chocolate Hobnob.

Shortly afterwards Grandma reappeared. Her interview – which had been taped, she told me later – had been short.

'Hardly enough time to drink my tea,' she complained.

'So what did they want?' I asked. 'What had you done?'

'Me?' she laughed. 'Nothing at all, unless you count knowing Malcolm McConnell a crime. It seems the police have been after him for ages for passing dud cheques and have been camped out in his house answering his telephone. When I phoned they thought I might possibly be an accomplice, so they decided to lay in wait for me. They just didn't expect my granddaughter and a daft dog to turn up as well. Though you could have been a cover, I suppose.' And she laughed. 'Bit of an adventure really.'

I laughed too. 'But how come they let you go so quickly? Didn't they have lots of questions?'

'Oh yes,' said Grandma. 'But when I said my lawyer was your mum, and they phoned her to check . . .'

'They phoned Mum?' I gasped. 'She knows you were arrested. *We* were arrested. She knows we're at the police station . . .'

Oh no, I thought, it would probably have been better if Grandma *had* been an Australian spy, after all!

22

You know that uncomfortable silence there is when an adult is about to give you a ticking-off, and they're just building up to it, deciding what words to say that will make you squirm most.

Well, there was one of these silences when Grandma and I arrived home.

To say Mum's face was like thunder is putting it too mildly. It looked like it had been chipped out of granite. Her brows were down, her jaw was clenched and I was sure I could hear her teeth grind and her fillings loosen.

But Grandma and I were ready. We had planned our defensive strategy on the train on the way home.

'I think we should treat the episode lightly,' said Grandma. 'Like it didn't really worry us. Like we thought it was a big adventure, and who'd have thought we'd be arrested by the police on a windy Saturday afternoon? Ha ha.'

I nodded. 'You don't think we should appear too traumatized.'

'No,' said Grandma. 'Are you feeling traumatized, Abby?' Grandma was concerned.

'A bit,' I confessed. 'If traumatized means a wobbly tum and a kind of hollow feeling inside.'

'You could be,' said Grandma. 'Or it could be hunger. We could stop for a hamburger on the way home, if you like?'

I shook my head. 'Better get straight home. Mum's expecting us. That WPC said she would phone her to say what train we'd be on.'

'You're right,' said Grandma. 'Better go straight home.'

'And get it over with,' I said.

'But we're not traumatized,' said Grandma.

'No,' I agreed. 'Not traumatized. Got that, Benson?'

But Benson was asleep at Grandma's feet. I think it was safe to say he definitely wasn't traumatized.

Mum, however, was a different matter.

When we arrived home she asked us first if we were all right. We were, as previously decided. Next she asked us what we wanted for tea. We settled for vegetarian chilli. She put that in the oven and asked us to sit down and tell her *exactly* what had happened.

We did, as previously rehearsed.

Then she gave us the row we knew was coming. Grandma got the worst of it. Not fit to be allowed out with children, always in trouble, what kind of grandparent couldn't be trusted with grandchildren etc etc etc. Grandma sat quietly through it. So did I, as previously agreed.

'Your mum will be angry,' Grandma had said. 'Mostly through worry and anxiety. We'll try not to make it any worse.'

But somehow our silence did.

Dumb insolence, Mrs Jackson calls it. But it wasn't that kind of silence, though Mum didn't seem to realize. She went on and on till even her best mate, Benson, had had enough and crawled under the table after giving her one of his most reproachful looks.

We ate our veggie chilli in silence, and silence reigned till Mum went upstairs to her study to do some work.

'That's it then, Grandma,' I sighed. 'No more Saturday trips to look for a man for Mum. We've been banned.'

Grandma snorted. 'Nonsense. What day is it today?'

'Saturday, of course,' I said, puzzled.

'And what is your mum doing?'

'She's in her study, working.'

'Exactly,' said Grandma. 'She's still a young woman, yet she's in her study working on a Saturday night when she should be out having fun. It's not natural. It's not right. Operation Boyfriend, Abby, is more important than ever. We can't give it up now.'

'Of course not,' I said. 'How stupid of me to think so. How wimpish. But how are we going to manage without Mum finding out, and putting you, old Belle and the crocodile boots on the next plane back to Oz?'

'Dunno,' grinned Grandma. 'But I'll think of something.'

That's exactly what I was afraid of!

23

Grandma and I decided to play it cool for a few days to let things settle down.

'Just let life take its natural course,' said Grandma.

It sounded like a good idea to me. Unfortunately, just when you need a quiet life, life has a nasty habit of turning round and biting you on the bum. And it was all because of the school bus.

I never ever thought of the school bus as something I could be fond of. In fact, I spent most of my time nearly missing it in the morning. I was convinced it came early just to catch me out. As I got to the front gate I could see it coming round the corner. I always had to race it to the bus stop. It could see me running full pelt, but did it slow down? It did not. It speeded up. I was sure the driver was in the pay of Belinda Fishcake, or was at least her mad uncle. I was sure she enjoyed seeing me look like a scruffy beetroot each morning as I stumbled on. I was sure it made her feel good to be sitting there, every hair in place, perfectly turned out.

'You look a mess,' she told me, as once more I leapt on to the bus as it started pulling away. 'Why on earth don't you just get up ten minutes earlier in the morning?'

'Why don't you just mind your own business,' I snarled, as I looked for an empty seat. But there was only one, beside Fishcake.

I had two choices. I could sit beside her or I could stand. I sat, puffed out from my exertions.

'Do you enjoy looking like a scarecrow?' asked Belinda, not minding her own business one little bit. 'Is it some kind of statement? *We* all reckon you're just too lazy to be bothered, actually.'

' "We" being the Beelines, I suppose.'

'And others.'

'What others?'

'Well, Andy Gray for a start. He was just asking me the other day why you always look like Worzel Gummidge's much scruffier younger sister.'

'No, he wasn't,' I said, stung.

'Ask him yourself,' shrugged Belinda.

She knew I wouldn't.

'I have more important things to do than spend my time preening and worrying about clothes,' I said, trying to sound convincing.

'So you won't be going to the school disco, then?' sneered Belinda.

'Haven't decided,' I said. But I had. Velvet and I had been talking about it for weeks. She was going to wear a lilac and silver salwar khameez, a Punjabi suit. I was going to wear – well I didn't quite know yet. I had looked in a few shop windows, but hadn't seen anything I'd liked. I seemed to be all arms, legs, teeth and hair at the moment. Nothing ever fitted properly. Clothes either gaped at the neck or the arm holes or my ankles stuck out beneath the trousers. I looked like ... I looked like Worzel Gummidge's much scruffier younger sister. I hadn't mentioned the disco at home yet because Mum would immediately want to take me shopping. She never likes anything I like, so we'd end up with something neither of us liked, and it would hang in the wardrobe till it was time to take it to the charity shop.

Then Belinda dropped her bombshell.

'Well,' she smirked, as the bus drew up at the school stop. 'I'm probably going to the disco with Andy. I've had *so* many requests, but I think I'll choose him.' And she gave a little self-satisfied smile and swung off the bus.

My jaw dropped so far I nearly tripped over it. I stumbled off behind her.

Andy! How could he? Didn't he know what she was like? Couldn't he see through her silly ways? Didn't he know she was only playing with his affections ... *oh, help!* I would have to stop reading these silly romances from the local library. I was was beginning to sound just like them! In the end I settled for ... Boys! Huh! Idiots!

That wasn't the only bombshell that day. Mr Doig announced at assembly that, owing to some more cutbacks, the school bus that served the area where I lived would be taken off at the end of the month.

There was a gasp of shock, mostly from me. How would I get to school? Mum drove, but in the opposite direction, and usually left before me. There were no trains, and Mum insisted the roads were too busy for me to ride my bike. So that left . . . walking. *walking*???

'*Strewth!*'

Forget romances. Now I was beginning to sound like Grandma.

24

'You'll just have to walk then,' said Mum. 'You'll just have to get up much earlier in the morning and walk.'

'But I'll have a heavy rucksack! And what if it's raining?' I protested.

'It may have escaped your notice, Abigail,' said Mum, 'but human beings don't actually dissolve in water. Their skin is waterproof, and, with the advent of modern technology, so is their rainwear. You can wear your anorak.'

This was the final insult. Nobody wears anoraks to school. It's decidedly uncool. And anyway, my anorak is pink with fluorescent stripes. Mum bought it for me. Surprise surprise!

'Walking's good for you.' Grandma was on Mum's side. 'I always used to walk to school when I was little. We didn't have such a thing as a school bus when I was your age.'

'I walked to school too,' said Mum, sounding very superior.

'Your school was at the foot of the road, Eva,' said Grandma. 'You could fall out of bed and into the playground. There's a difference.'

'It's the principle,' muttered Mum.

'Back on the sheep farm, I went everywhere on horseback,' smiled Grandma. 'I had a lovely little mare called Dusty.'

'Wow, that would be great,' I said, and looked hopeful, but Mum squashed that idea immediately.

'We are not, repeat *not*,' she said, 'buying a horse.'

'Why not?' I said, winding her up. 'It could live in the back garden and sleep in the shed with old Belle. And just think of how good the manure would be for your roses. I could park the horse in the bike shed at school, and perhaps that nice WPC we met when we were arrested could get me a spare fluorescent jacket with POLICE on the back. That way I would be safe in traffic. No one's going to run over a police horse. What do you think?'

'I think Mrs Jackson's right about your over-active imagination,' said Mum. 'It'll do you no harm to walk to school, with your young legs.'

'Wait a minute,' frowned Grandma. 'After the bus drops you at school, Abby, isn't that the same one that comes back this way and takes the pensioners into town?'

'Uh huh,' I nodded. 'Why?'

'Well,' said Grandma, 'their legs aren't young any more and they certainly can't carry heavy bags of shopping. This won't do. They can't take that bus off. They can't do that to the pensioners. I'll have to see about this.'

Good old Grandma. I knew I could rely on her.

Grandma had a word with Mrs Polanski and the following evening our sitting room was full of pensioners again.

'Hope you don't mind, Eva,' said Grandma, as Mum retreated upstairs to her study. 'There won't be any dancing this time. This is too important. We must exercise people power – or rather, pensioner power.'

'Just don't make too much noise,' muttered Mum. 'I've got work to do. What about your homework, Abby?'

'Done it,' I said. Well, I had. Maybe not all of it, and maybe not very well, but I wanted to see pensioner power in action. I had visions of super-powered zimmer frames charging like chariots into action; hollowed-out walking sticks used like giant pea shooters; and hearing aids tuned to receive battle commands. I could see Grandma astride a horse, leading the infantry. Except, could it be *infant*ry if it was old people? I'd have to ask Mrs Jackson about that.

First, Grandma got them all fired up about the injustice of the situation.

'You've paid your taxes all your lives,' she said. 'You are entitled to some consideration. No one

98

should be able to make you prisoners in your own homes because you have no transport.'

There were cries of 'Quite right' and 'Filthy swines' etc.

Then there were several suggestions about how to make the bus company change its mind about taking off the bus.

'Pelt them with flour bombs,' said Mr Hobbs, who was in his second childhood and loving every minute of it.

'Pelt them with rotten eggs,' said Mrs Hobbs, who always agreed with her husband.

'We could write and ask them to keep the bus running,' said Miss Flack, who was rather shy.

'They won't listen. Never do, these power-mad johnnies,' said Major Knotts, who still had the handlebar moustache he had grown during the Second World War.

'We could make placards and walk around outside with them,' said Mrs Byng.

'I'm not very good at walking now,' said Mrs Polanski. 'I'm only good at sitting.'

'That's it!' said Grandma. 'That's what we'll do. We'll have a sit-in. We can all do that. We'll go to the bus company's head office and we'll sit there till they change their minds. Nice peaceful protest. To begin with, anyway.'

'Good idea,' everyone agreed. 'But we'll need to be prepared. We'll need flasks of tea.'

'I'll organize the flasks,' said Major Knotts. 'Got

a load in the shed from when I had the army surplus shop.'

'I'll make the sandwiches,' said Mrs Polanski. 'Just wait till you taste my Polish sausage!'

'I could bake some fairy cakes with a little cherry on the top,' said Miss Flack. 'I'm quite good at that.'

'I'd still like to pelt them with flour bombs,' said Mr Hobbs.

'And rotten eggs,' said his wife.

'Let's try the sit-in first,' said Grandma gently. 'We can keep the flour and eggs in reserve.'

I cleared my throat to speak.

'If you like, I could do the placards and walk about outside after school. I could get some friends to help. The bus affects us too.'

'Good idea,' said Grandma. 'Now if that's all settled, I think it's time for tea. Organizing pensioner power makes me really hungry. See what's in the cupboard, Abby. I could eat a barbied bush snake.'

We were fresh out of roasted rattlers so Grandma and her pals had to be content with chocolate biscuits. They gummed down a whole week's supply; especially Mum's favourites with the minty bits in them.

Finally, after a few stories about the good old days, when Adam was a boy and Eve certainly didn't wear skirts that hardly covered next week's washing, the pensioners went home and prepared for battle.

Grandma and I cleared away the tea things and Benson sniffed about looking for any crumbs the pensioners might have missed. No chance. These were piranha pensioners. Not a morsel escaped them. Benson slumped down on the carpet, dejected, but perked up when he heard Mum come downstairs. He greeted her like he hadn't seen her in years, never mind an hour or so ago.

'Down, Benson,' said Mum, which Benson obviously thought meant leap all over me, knock me off my feet, and cover me in slobber, Benson.

'That dog knows everything you say, Eva,' grinned Grandma.

'Maybe he's deaf,' I said. 'He certainly never did anything Frau Gripperknickers said at the dog-training classes. When she said "Sit" he stood up. When she said "Stay" he galloped all round the room, and when she said "Heel" he lifted his leg against the chair where she'd left her coat. Perhaps that's why she asked us to leave.'

'Expelled from dog-training classes, Benson,' said Mum, fondly stroking his ears. 'How could you?'

Benson licked her hand and wagged his tail, sending the potted geranium on the coffee table flying. Grandma caught it expertly. I bet she'd be good at cricket. I had an old cricket bat somewhere I usually kept for warding off mad axe murderers. Perhaps we could have a game some time. Grandma and me, that is.

Mum got up. 'Come on, Benson,' she said. 'Let's

go walkies and get some fresh air. Put the kettle on, Abby, it's been a long hard day. When I come back I'll treat myself to a nice cup of tea and one of those minty chocolate biscuits.'

Oops!

25

I told Mad Max, the Art teacher, about the bus problem, and he very kindly gave me some old card that Velvet and I could make into placards. I asked Belinda Fishcake if she wanted to help too, but she declined.

'I'll just get a lift to school in Daddy's new Merc,' she said.

I made a face. I didn't have a dad, let alone one with a Merc.

I got some red felt-tip pens and wrote SAVE OUR SCHOOL BUS on the card in big capitals. At least, that's what I meant to do, but the capitals were too big and the sign only read SAVE OUR SCHOO before I ran out of card. Velvet, of course, with her logical mind, had measured everything out first and had made a perfect placard.

'Turn the card over and write smaller on the other side,' she said. 'Rough the words out in pencil first, then it's easy to correct mistakes.'

I did as instructed and made a perfect placard

too, but it looked a bit boring so I drew a bus on it as well, with little matchstick people inside. Then I drew some cars and lorries, and an accident. That led to a traffic jam and some police cars and an ambulance. Finally I put in some rescue helicopters.

Velvet sighed when she saw it.

'Now you can hardly see the writing,' she said. 'There's so much else to look at.'

'You're right,' I said. 'I got carried away.'

'You and your imagination,' grinned Velvet. She made all the rest of the signs herself and she doesn't even use the bus.

A few more kids offered to parade with placards and the protest was staged for the following Monday when we had a day off school.

Grandma had phoned the local newspaper to tell them what was going to happen so, when the pensioners arrived at the bus company's head office with their flasks and their sandwiches, and we arrived with our placards, the press were there to witness it. Grandma made sure they knew exactly what it was all about. She made a little speech in the rather grand foyer of the bus company's head office.

'People before profit,' she announced. We had worked hard on that sound bite, and she repeated it several times thoughout her little speech. The pensioners were all there with more zimmers and walking sticks than I remembered. Even Major Knotts arrived on two sticks he certainly didn't need. They knew a thing or two about publicity, these old folk.

The bus company were embarrassed. They sent a 'spokesman' out to talk to the press. He waffled on about viability.

'Vi who?' asked Mrs Polanski. 'Do I know her? Does she work here?'

The reply was drowned out by laughter and our chanting about saving our school bus. We had a great time till the police arrived. They moved us on because of an accident. It wasn't a bad accident, just a line of cars and lorries bumping into each other because someone at the front had slowed down to watch our protest and the others hadn't. So there *was* a traffic jam, some police cars, and an ambulance. No helicopters, although the nice WPC who had chatted to us when we were arrested arrived.

'You two again,' she grinned. 'This is getting to be a habit.'

We got on to the national news. Not the top story, but that little heart-warming one at the end when the newscaster smiles and says, 'Finally, we have a story about how a pensioners' and pupils' protest about their bus got them into a bit of a jam.' And there was the picture of the traffic jam and Grandma saying her bit about 'People before profit' and me and the other kids marching up and down with our placards.

Mum shook her head.

'We used to have a quiet life in this house,' she said. 'No one getting arrested. No one on the six o'clock news.'

Grandma made a face. 'I couldn't just sit back, Eva. Not when it involved the old folk.'

Mum smiled. 'No, you're quite right. People have a right to protest. This is a democracy after all.'

Hmm, democracy, I thought. What exactly did that mean? I sneaked off to have a quick look in the dictionary.

Democracy – A form of government in which the supreme power is vested in the people.

Quite right too. Pensioner power. Pupil power. People power. Yeah!

Then the phone rang and Mum got up to answer it.

'Probably someone ringing to congratulate us on our demo,' said Grandma.

'Or Hollywood offering us a part in their latest blockbuster movie about democracy.' It was one of my words now.

It was neither of those.

Mum came back looking a bit white-faced. 'That was the senior partner,' she said. 'Asking me if I was aware that our firm were the bus company's lawyers, and what was I doing letting my mother and daughter become involved in a public demonstration.'

I opened my mouth to say something smart about democracy, then I shut it again. Sometimes, you just can't win.

26

Because of all the publicity, the bus company agreed to have another look at their bus routes and timetables.

'Good for you, Abby,' Andy congratulated me in the school playground. 'That was really cool, organizing that demo.'

'Yeah,' I said, and was going to take all the credit till my conscience got the better of me. 'Actually it was mostly Grandma's doing, though she doesn't think we've won yet. She reckons the bus company is just lying low till the fuss dies down.'

Andy nodded. 'Well, let me know if you need any help. I'll come along next time.'

'OK,' I grinned.

Was it wrong now to hope there'd be a next time? I could see myself marching up and down beside Andy. Tirelessly, like a suffragette. Hey, that was an idea. I could chain myself to some railings, or if they were in short supply, a tree or a radiator. I would be on TV and be famous, and

Andy would be even more impressed.

Belinda (Eyes in the Back of her Head) Fishcake saw me talking to Andy and came rushing over.

'Hi, Belinda,' said Andy. 'I was just congratulating Abby on her demo at the bus company.'

'Oh yes,' said Belinda. 'I was so sorry I couldn't manage to come, Abby. But, next time, of course, I'll be there.'

'Me too,' said Andy.

'We'll go together, Andy,' said Belinda, clutching his arm. 'It'll be fun.'

Andy smiled. I grimaced and walked away.

How does she do it? I thought. One minute I'm chatting to Andy, the next she's practically got a date with him. It's just not fair.

I was in a grumpy mood all day because of it, and moaned about it to Grandma when I got home.

Grandma was sympathetic. 'Some females are just like that, Abby. They don't want something till they see someone else with it. But we'll sort out Belinda Fishcake, don't you worry. First, though, we've got to carry on with Operation Boyfriend for your mum.'

'But how?' I asked. 'We're banned from going anywhere in case we get arrested again.'

'I know,' said Grandma. 'But I think we might get away with this – Mrs Polanski wants to visit her old neighbour in Newburgh, and has asked me to go with her on the bus since she's not too steady on her feet. You could come too to keep an eye on both of us. Your mum couldn't object to that. It's a mission of mercy.'

'Newburgh!' I said excitedly. 'Isn't that where . . .'

'Colin Birkmyre lives,' grinned Grandma. 'Number two on our list. We can slip away while Mrs Polanski's at her friend's and check him out.'

'You, Grandma,' I said, 'are really sneaky.'

'I know,' said Grandma. 'Good, isn't it?'

27

It took Mrs Polanski ages to get ready for the outing. She had to check all the doors and windows in her house twice, to make sure they were properly locked. She had to check the gas was turned off and that she hadn't left a tap running anywhere. And we were at least fifteen minutes looking for her keys (which were in the lock) and her glasses (which were on her head underneath her hat). But we caught the bus. Just.

'Come on, hurry along there, Granny,' said the bus driver, who had a whiny voice and ears weighed down by the contents of a small silver mine. 'I haven't got all day.'

Mrs Polanski raised herself up to her formidable four feet ten inches.

'I am not your granny, young man,' she informed him. 'And if I was you'd have better manners. Now you will wait until I am properly seated before you start this bus or I will deliberately fall over, break my hip, and sue both you and the bus company for all you have, including your earrings!'

'Mrs Polanski's really got the hang of pensioner power,' I whispered to Grandma.

Grandma winked. 'I think we may have started a small revolution.'

We sat down and the bus moved off, gently. We'd only gone half a mile or so when Mrs Polanski reached into her shopping bag and took out a flask of tea and some sandwiches. We had a picnic on the bus. An hour later we got off the bus in the middle of an area of neat bungalows. We found Havelock Terrace and took Mrs Polanski to visit her friend, Monica. Monica was delighted to see us and immediately produced tea and sandwiches, which she insisted we ate. She also insisted we ate large slices of home-made fruit cake. By this stage, Grandma and I were so full that, when Monica wasn't looking, we fed the fruit cake to her Cairn terrier, Sally. Sally was so fat, her stomach brushed the carpet when she moved. I think she ate a lot of fruit cake. Then Grandma and I excused ourselves.

'We'll just go for a little walk,' Grandma told the two old ladies, 'to stretch our legs and let you chat in peace.'

'Don't be too long,' warned Mrs Polanski. 'We don't want to miss the bus back.'

We promised faithfully and set off. Grandma had brought a street directory with her, showing that Colin Birkmyre's house was only about half a mile away.

'Come on,' said Grandma, and set off at a brisk trot.

The modern bungalows gave way to semis with neat gardens and the odd garden gnome fishing hopefully in a plastic pond. Then we came to one house which stood out from the rest. It had pink frilly curtains at the windows, and late flowering pink roses in the garden, with pink stepping stones arranged daintily between them. A sign at the pink front door said ROSE AND COLIN LIVE HERE.

'This doesn't look promising,' frowned Grandma.

She rang the doorbell which played *Lily the Pink* till the door was answered by a round-shouldered, balding man of about Grandma's age. He was wearing a flowery pink apron.

'Colin?' Grandma was incredulous.

'Yes,' said the man, but before he could say any more an imperious voice from within shouted, 'Who is it? If they're selling something, we don't want it. If they're collecting money, we don't give it, and if it's her from number thirty-five, no, I haven't seen her mangy cat!'

'It's none of those, Colin,' said Grandma. 'It's Aphrodite. Remember, we were students together, long time ago. I was in the area and thought I would look you up.'

'Aphrodite?' Colin's pale face broke into a smile. 'Gosh, I haven't seen you in, how many years is it . . . ?'

'Who *is* it, Colin?' demanded the voice again. 'Come in and close the door, there's a terrible draught.'

'It's just an old friend, dear,' said Colin.

'Friend?' said the voice. '*FRIEND*? Of yours?' And the voice from within materialized into female form and came to the door.

To say Mrs Birkmyre was large would be lying. She was *enormous*. Imagine a mound of car tyres under a pink frock and you'll come close. Her eyes were close too. Like two black raisins in a lump of lard. The raisins eyed us suspiciously. 'What do you want?' she asked, marginally more friendly than a rabid Rottweiler.

'Just a chat with an old friend,' said Grandma. 'Colin and I were students together. I've been out of the country for a number of years and thought I'd come to see him.'

'Well, you've seen him now,' she said. 'We don't do chats, and we don't do old friends.' And she yanked Colin back inside and closed the door.

Grandma and I stood there for a moment, shocked. Then, Grandma smiled sadly. 'Poor old Colin. To think he used to risk life and limb climbing tall buildings to hang up peace banners. Whatever happened to him? Come on, Abby, let's have another little walk before we pick up Mrs Polanski. We'll need to work up an appetite from somewhere, I think she has more sandwiches for the journey home.'

Grandma was a little quiet on the way back on the bus. When Mrs Polanski nodded off I asked her what was wrong.

'I was just remembering how Colin used to be,' she said. 'So full of fun and mischief. Now look at him.'

'We never did find out if he had any sons,' I said. 'But perhaps that's just as well.'

Grandma agreed. 'Only thing is, Abby, that just leaves one on our list. There's only Charlie Anderson left.'

28

The day of the school disco drew near and I still had nothing to wear. I decided I would have to tell Mum about the disco and do the dreaded shop trail with her.

Mum was delighted I was going.

'You'll enjoy it,' she said. 'We'll go out on Saturday and find you something suitable to wear.'

It was that 'suitable' that worried me. I had a vision of me dressed up like Heidi, all smock top and embroidery with my hair in plaits, or in something long and flowery like a refugee from *The Little House on the Prairie*. Anything Mum bought me certainly wouldn't be high fashion. Not that I'm particularly worried about that, though deep down I suppose I wanted to look more or less like the rest of the world. But I knew Mum would have none of that.

Neither would Velvet.

'I won't blend in with the crowd,' she said, 'in a Punjabi suit. I'll look different, but I'll look like myself; not like some kind of clone.'

Whose side was she on anyway!

Saturday started off badly. I like a lie-in on a Saturday, but Mum wanted to go to the shops early to be sure of getting a parking place. She woke me up before the birds had even yawned. Certainly before dawn had cracked.

I'm not good in the morning. I stood under the shower in a daze, still in my nightie. Then I skooshed on hairspray instead of deodorant. Cleaning my teeth with the zit cream was not a good idea. It tasted horrible. Not a good start to the day.

Mum was waiting for me at the foot of the stairs, toe tapping impatiently. 'You're not going out like that,' she said.

'Like what? Comfy tracky bottoms and a T-shirt, what's wrong with that?'

Everything, apparently.

I had to go back upstairs and change into something respectable – i.e. something Mum had bought me. I came down again wearing my sullen expression and a white blouse and blue skirt.

'Where is the matching waistcoat?' asked Mum.

Waistcoat!!! I could only hope I wouldn't meet anyone I knew.

But of course I did.

Mum manoeuvred the car into the very last space in the car park – beside the smelly bins where nobody likes to park – and opened the car doors carefully. There wasn't much room to squeeze out. Then, would you believe it, she tidied me up before we set off for the shopping mall. Mum headed for the big department store where she buys her 'power' suits. I headed for the teenage shops. Mum yanked me back.

'We'll look in here first,' she said.

'No point,' I said. 'That's for old folk. My shops are this way.'

'There's nothing in those shops that will do.'

'How do you know if we don't even look . . .'

On and on it went, in the middle of the shopping mall, before I'd even tried anything on.

That was when Belinda Fishcake passed, wearing tracky bottoms and a T-shirt; and so was her mum.

'I like your outfit, Abby,' Belinda giggled. 'It's *so* you.' And she flicked back a strand of long gleaming hair and smiled a perfect, braceless smile.

I glowered at her. Mum glowered at me, and smiled at Mrs Fisher. 'Children!' she said.

Children, indeed!

Things went from bad to worse. Nothing I liked, Mum liked. Nothing Mum liked would I have been seen dead in a doorway wearing; so after trailing round and round, shop after shop, we returned to the car, empty-handed and not speaking to each other.

The car park had emptied and Mum's car was left sitting on its own, a large dent in its back end.

A large dent???

'Look at that!' yelled Mum. 'Who did that? It wasn't there before.' She ran over to have a closer look. The offside rear light was broken and little bits of red glass littered the ground. Mum stamped her foot in anger. For a moment I thought she was going to lose it completely and have a tantrum like I used to have when I was two. Apparently I used to lie on the floor and drum my heels on the carpet if I didn't get my own way. I wondered if that would work now.

Mum gathered herself together.

'Let's get home,' she said, through gritted teeth.

We got into the car and she reversed out over the broken glass.

'There goes a tyre as well,' I nearly said, but didn't.

Maybe I'm becoming more mature, I thought. That's a word I've recently added to my collection, but I don't like it so much now I've discovered it's also used to describe pongy old cheese.

Grandma was waiting for us when we got home. One look at our faces, and *she* didn't say anything either. I guess she's mature too. She just went and put the kettle on and made a pot of tea. I went upstairs and put on my comfy tracky bottoms and a T-shirt. What a day!

29

For some weeks now, Grandma had been getting letters from Australia. They always cheered her up. When she came downstairs in the morning and saw a letter with an Australian stamp on it, her face broke into a big grin, and she took the letter back upstairs to read it. She appeared again, all smiles. She never actually said what was in the letters or who they were from, and one day I was so curious I asked her.

'Just an old friend,' she said vaguely. 'It's nice to keep up with old friends.'

But I know she never wrote back. She wrote to our MP about the bus problem; she wrote to the council about the holes in the pavement outside Mrs Polanski's front door, and that was it. I know because I posted the letters at Velvet's parents' little post office, but I never ever posted any letters to Australia.

I mentioned this to Mum.

'Perhaps she writes them and posts them herself

while you're at school,' said Mum. 'Though it's really none of your business.'

I knew it wasn't, but it niggled at me somehow. Grandma would be the first to tell me off if I didn't write back to a friend.

Curiosity finally got the better of me – again – so the next time I was in the little post office, I asked Velvet's mum, 'Does Grandma ever come in here to post letters to Australia, Mrs Guha?'

Velvet's mum shook her head and her long black ponytail swung from side to side.

'No, I don't think so. Sometimes she comes in for sweets if she's meeting you from school, but that's all. She's a nice lady, your grandma. I like her.'

'I like her too,' I smiled, but I still thought there was something odd going on.

'I haven't forgotten about that nice Indian doctor for your mum,' Mrs Guha went on. 'I might have some news soon.'

'Oh good,' I said, but my mind was on other things.

BIG MISTAKE.

Two nights later, while the three of us were sitting watching a wildlife programme about orang-utans, the phone rang. Mum got up to answer it.

'Hullo,' she said absently, one eye still on the TV. Then she stood up straight and her back went rigid, the way it does when she's really annoyed.

'Somebody selling double glazing, probably,' muttered Grandma.

'Or new kitchens,' I said.

Mum listened very intently for a few moments then said in her tight little lawyer's voice, 'Well, thank you very much for your concern, but I'm afraid you have been misinformed. A meeting would not be useful as I have no intention of taking the matter further. I'm sorry you have been troubled.' And she put the phone down. She strode across to the television and switched it off.

'Oi,' Grandma and I said. 'We were watching that.'

Mum wasn't listening. She was angry, furious, mad as a cut snake, as Grandma would say.

'That was Mrs Guha,' she spat out, 'offering to arrange a meeting for me with a nice Indian doctor she knows. Apparently she heard that I was needing a husband. Apparently it's all over the neighbourhood that I want to get married again, but can't find a suitable man. Now I wonder where that idea could have come from?'

Grandma and I should have won an Oscar for how innocent we managed to look, but Mum wasn't fooled.

'I don't know what idiotic mischief you two have been up to,' she said, 'but you will kindly stop meddling in my affairs.'

'You're not *having* any affairs, Eva,' Grandma pointed out. 'That's the problem.'

'*You're* the problem!' yelled Mum. 'I was fine till you got here. *We* were fine till you got here. Now keep your nose out of my business or you can find yourself somewhere else to live.'

And she banged out of the room and thudded upstairs to sulk. Much like I would have done.

'She doesn't mean it,' I said. 'She'll calm down. She's just upset.'

'I know,' sighed Grandma. 'Some people are very difficult to help.'

'Shall we just call our secret project off, then?' I asked.

'No,' said Grandma. 'We set out to do something and we'll see it through. We still have one name left to look up.'

'But what if Mum really does throw you out?'

'We'll cross that bridge when we come to it,' said Grandma.

30

Mothers aren't supposed to go off in a huff. Children go off in a huff. Mothers are supposed to know better.

Mine didn't. She went in a definite huff, and, when she did speak, she was icily polite.

'Pass me the milk, please.'

'No, thank you, I do not wish to have a chocolate biscuit.'

'Kindly bring your dirty laundry downstairs before you go to school.'

It was ridiculous.

'How long is she going to keep this up?' I asked Grandma.

'Who knows?' she said. 'She was really good at it as a child. It could go on for days.'

'Tell me what Mum was like as a child,' I said.

Grandma's face softened.

'She was lovely. Happy and bright – till she didn't get her own way, then the sparks would fly. Tantrums, yelling, banging doors, that kind of thing.'

'Not much change, then,' I grinned.

Grandma smiled. 'She always found it hard to admit when she was wrong. Still does.'

'Who does she get that from?' I suddenly felt very mature again.

'Me, of course,' admitted Grandma. 'Your grandad always said we were very alike in that respect – that was the trouble.'

'We've got trouble now all right,' I said. '*And* the school disco's next week *and* I've got nothing to wear. I'm not asking Mum again. Perhaps I just won't go. That would be easier.'

'Don't be silly,' said Grandma. 'There must be something you can wear. What about some of my sixties' dresses?'

'I thought about that,' I said, 'but something Velvet said put me off. She said I should be myself and not want to look like anyone else. If I wore one of your dresses I would look like you, Grandma. You said so yourself.'

'You're right,' said Grandma, 'and so is Velvet. She's a sensible girl, and a good friend. Wait a minute though, I have an idea.'

She went to the sideboard and brought back some paper and a pen.

'Draw the kind of outfit you would like to wear.'

'*Draw* it? I can't draw it!'

'Make a sketch,' said Grandma. 'You don't have to be Michelangelo to make a sketch.'

I thought for a moment. What *did* I want to wear?

Trousers? Definitely trousers. Jeans? No. Flares? No. Straight-legged? Maybe. Cropped? Yes. Cropped black trousers.

'Good,' said Grandma. 'What about the top half?'

Hmm. Strappy top? No. Skinny rib? No. T-shirt? Maybe gold blouse? Yes. Gold blouse. So I drew that too.

'Well that doesn't look too outrageous to me,' said Grandma. 'We'll get the material tomorrow and make it.'

'Make it?' I squeaked. 'Oh no, I don't think so.'

Now I was going to go straight from *The Little House on the Prairie* to looking like an extra in *Oliver Twist*.

'Don't worry,' Grandma laughed. '*I'm* not going to make it. Miss Flack will. She used to make clothes for Harrods.'

'But Miss Flack's ancient,' I said. 'How will she know what I want?'

'Just because people are old, Abby, doesn't mean they have lost all the skills they acquired in their lifetime. Miss Flack will know what you want because *you* know, now you've drawn it.'

Grandma made it sound so simple, but I wasn't convinced. I was sure I would turn up at the disco looking like an Oxfam reject.

I thought it best to tell Mum what we were doing, but I needn't have bothered.

'Please yourself,' she said. 'You and your grandmother always do. I want no part of it.'

But she did. Whenever Grandma and I talked about it, she listened, although she pretended not to. Grandma showed her the material we'd bought, but she just shrugged, so we carried on anyway.

Miss Flack lived a fifteen-minute walk away, but only five minutes if you crossed by the field at the end of the road.

'Should we go through the field, Grandma? It's got a Keep Out notice on it,' I said, as we climbed over the five-barred gate and set off across the grass.

'Don't know why,' said Grandma, as the big black bull came out from behind some trees and thundered towards us.

There was no way back.

Grandma and I raced for the safety of the other side. We definitely did a personal best on that run. You do, if a ton of angry pot roast is snorting at your heels.

'Now I know why the notice is up,' said Grandma, collapsing in a heap on the grass and panting like a . . . like a grandma.

But I noticed she didn't say, 'Sorry I put you in danger, Abby. I was wrong to bring you across the field.' She and Mum *were* alike, after all.

If Miss Flack thought we looked a bit hot and dusty when we arrived she didn't say. She just invited us into her tiny sitting room and offered us tea.

'It's so nice to see you,' she said. 'I don't have many visitors.'

I looked around me. If I was worried about Miss Flack's expertise with a needle, I needn't have been. Her house was filled with beautiful cushions and tapestries. But could she do a fabulous disco outfit?

Of course she could. In her sleep. One hand tied behind her back, and with a blunt needle. Before my eyes the shy Miss Flack disappeared and the professional one took her place. First she measured me, then looked at the material we had bought.

'Good choice,' she said. 'Always buy the best material you can afford. It looks better in the end.'

Then she talked to me about what I wanted. She really listened while I wittered about looking tall and elegant, and not like a beanpole. After a while she made some suggestions of her own. Would I like some little diamantés down the sides of the trousers, and a little matching scatter on the shoulder of my blouse? How about the gold and black material twisted into little braids to go through my hair? What did I think of the tiniest little black and gold bag to hang at my waist for my money or lip gloss? I thought it all sounded wonderful. This whole outfit was going to be fantastic. It was just going to be so totally *me*.

Four days later Miss Flack handed it in. She didn't look hot and dusty, so I think she must have walked round to our house the long way.

Even Mum was impressed by the black and gold

number. She was back talking to us again. She'd lost her car keys one morning and was going to be late for work, so she had to ask us help her look, and that was that.

I couldn't wait to try the outfit on. I raced upstairs with it. It fitted perfectly. Like it had been made for me! The trousers made my legs look really long and elegant, and the blouse – well, either my bosom had grown a bit or Miss Flack really *was* a genius.

I skipped downstairs to let everyone see.

'Fantastic,' said Grandma.

'Very nice,' said Mum.

'You look like a model,' said Miss Flack.

If I'd been chocolate I'd have eaten myself. I practised a few dance steps on the carpet and Mum went to get her purse.

'You've done a beautiful job, Miss Flack,' she said. 'What do I owe you?'

Miss Flack waved her away. 'You don't owe me anything,' she said. 'I was happy to do it – but I would be very pleased if Abby would come to visit again and tell me all about the disco.'

'Just try to stop me,' I said. 'The disco's going to be great now.'

I beamed. Grandma beamed. Mum beamed.

'You are so alike, you three,' smiled Miss Flack. 'You are so lucky to have each other.'

31

There wasn't much work done in school for the next couple of days; everyone was too busy thinking about the disco. Belinda Fishcake and the Beelines spent hours talking about what they were going to wear, how they were going to do their hair, what colour nail polish to put on. I just went about with a little smile on my face.

'What are *you* up to, Abigail Montgomery?' asked Fishcake one lunchtime. 'You're looking very pleased about something.'

'I'm not up to anything,' I said. 'I'm just a naturally happy person.'

'No you're not.' Fishcake was suspicious. 'You've usually got a face like a squashed frog.'

The Beelines tittered, 'Oh you're so funny, Belinda.'

But even they couldn't upset me. I just smiled at them. 'Clones,' I said, shook my head sadly and strolled away.

'What did she say?' muttered the Beelines.

'Phones?'

'Moans?'

'Bones?'

'Ignore her,' said Belinda. 'She's finally flipped. Now who's going to wear Strawberry Surprise lip gloss? I think it's a really yummy colour . . .'

The Friday evening of the disco arrived. I had stayed late at school helping to decorate the hall and had to rush to shower and change when I got home. I was standing there in my black trousers and gold blouse with Grandma fixing the braids in my hair and Mum fiddling with the bag at my waist when the phone rang.

Mum picked it up.

'It's for you,' she said. 'Some boy, sounded a bit shy.'

I took the phone.

'It's Andy,' said the voice in my ear.

'Hi, Andy.'

'Stand still!' muttered Mum. 'How am I supposed to fix this if you won't stand still?'

'I was wondering,' said Andy. 'I mean, I saw you in the hall this afternoon, helping with the disco lights . . . and I was wondering . . . I mean, does that mean you're going to the disco . . . ? not everyone is . . . but I thought since you were helping you must be going . . .'

'Yes, I'm going,' I said, puzzled. 'Aren't you?'

'Yes ... well ... yes, I'm going, and I just wondered ...'

'Yes?'

'Well, I just wondered ... if you would like to go with me. I know it's very late to ask you, but I didn't like to ask before, and now I realize it's probably too late, and you're probably going with someone else, so that's all right, so just forget I asked. OK?'

And he was about to ring off. IDIOT!!!

'Andy!' I yelled. 'Wait a minute.' Grandma got such a fright she yanked my hair and I yelled again.

'What is it?' asked Andy. 'Are you all right?'

'Fine,' I said. 'But, Andy – aren't you going to the disco with Belinda?'

'No,' said Andy, puzzled. 'Whatever gave you that idea?'

'Just something I heard,' I said. 'Well, in that case, I'd like to go with you.'

'You would?' It was Andy's turn to yell.

I held the phone away from my ear. 'I would.'

'Great!' said Andy. 'Dad's giving me a lift. Can we pick you up in half an hour?'

'OK,' I said, trying to sound casual, but I was grinning from ear to ear.

I rang off and looked at Grandma and Mum. They were grinning from ear to ear too.

'What?' I said. 'What?'

'Nothing!' they both said, and carried on grinning.

The disco was great great great. I had a really really really good time. The first really great bit was when Andy came to the front door to pick me up. He took one look at me and said exactly the right thing.

'You look fantastic!'

'So do you,' I said, and he did. He had on black jeans, a bright red shirt and he'd spiked his hair.

'Mum doesn't like my hair.'

'It's cool.'

'Thanks,' he said, 'but you *really* look amazing.'

'Thanks,' I said, like I was used to such great compliments.

Grown-up, or what?

The next really great bit was making 'our entrance'. Notice that word 'our'.

Belinda and the Beelines were standing near the door of the hall to check out what everyone was wearing. I could see their look of surprise when they saw my outfit, and their look of puzzlement when I appeared with Andy. So, just in case there was any doubt as to what was what, I took a leaf out of Belinda's book and did a little pretend stumble in my new black sandals.

'You all right, Abby?' said Andy, and put his arm round my waist.

'Fine, just these new shoes,' I lied.

I could see the Beelines nudge each other and begin to chatter like budgies. Belinda looked very annoyed.

'Hi,' I said, smiling sweetly as I passed them. 'Isn't this a really great disco, Clones?'

'Cones?' they said. 'Did she say cones? I'm sure she said cones.'

Clones or cones, it didn't matter. In their short, tight, spangly dresses, matching hair and nail polish, they all looked dead boring, anyway.

The next really great bit was everybody asking me where I got my outfit.

'Oh,' I said, airily. 'I have a friend who used to make clothes for Harrods. Now she's freelance.'

Well, it was *nearly* true.

The next really great bit was everyone asking me how long I'd been going out with Andy.

'Not long,' I said, and that really *was* true. At that point, by my reckoning, about fifty-two-and-a-half minutes.

The second last really great bit was Andy walking me to my front door and saying, 'I had a smashing time, Abby. Can I see you tomorrow?'

'At school?' I said, stupidly.

'Tomorrow's Saturday. I thought maybe we could go somewhere. Get a pizza or something.'

'OK,' I said, trying to play it cool while my heart played bongo drums in my chest.

'Goodnight then.'

'Goodnight then.'

'See you tomorrow.'

'See you tomorrow.'

And the last really great bit was lying in bed that

night going over and over it all again in my head. My very own action replay.

The disco was great great great. I had a really really really good time. Did I tell you that already?

32

'You're going out with a *boy*,' said Mum next morning when I told her I was meeting Andy in town. She made it sound like I was going out with a three-headed monster from the far side of the moon.

'It's not a *boy*,' I said. 'It's Andy. I went to the disco with him. You met him last night. His gran has a mad German shepherd who got expelled from dog-training classes same time as Benson. You liked him – Andy, that is.'

'Well, I don't know.' Mum was doubtful.

'There's nothing *to* know!' I said. 'We'll go and get a pizza or a knickerbocker glory. Then maybe we'll get a video and come back here.'

'Where are you going to get the money to do all that?'

'Well, it is pocket-money day, and I thought you might be feeling extra generous.'

'Well, I don't know . . .'

Two I don't knows in a row – Mum was sickening for something.

'Oh go on, Eva,' said Grandma. 'Give her some money and let her enjoy herself. Do her good to get away from us old fogies for a change.'

'*I'm* not an old fogey!' Mum was indignant.

Grandma shrugged. 'If you say so, Eva.'

Mum muttered under her breath and gave me extra pocket money.

'Now be careful,' she said.

I put on an angelic expression. 'I'll always cross the road with the green man, and I'll take my anorak in case it rains.'

'Don't be cheeky,' said Mum. 'You know what I mean.'

I did, and it included: Don't get carried off by aliens . . . Don't take any illegal substances . . . and don't get pregnant.

Who'd have thought going for a pizza could be so complicated?

In the end, Andy and I went to the Sea Life Centre to look at the sharks. We had a great time spotting which ones reminded us of our teachers. There was a really bossy one with a huge mouth who was a dead ringer for Mrs Jackson.

'Your over-active imagination will be the death of you, Abigail Montgomery,' I mimicked. 'You really must learn to curb it. When writing a factual piece you should not invent things to make it appear more interesting.'

'You sound just like her.' Andy was admiring. 'Let's see if there's one that looks like Mr Doig.'

We had a chocolate sundae each after that. We would have had two, but our money ran out. Then I swore Andy to secrecy and told him about Operation Boyfriend to find a man for Mum. 'It's very difficult to carry on with it now,' I said, 'because Mum's so cross about it all. Grandma and I can't get away on our own.'

Andy was thoughtful. 'What if I came too?' he said. 'There must be an aquarium or a wildlife centre where this Charles Anderson lives. Your grandma could pretend to go with us and could look up her old friend!'

'It might work. It's worth a try, but Mum's really suspicious. It's not easy having a lawyer as a mum.'

'You should try having a school teacher,' said Andy. 'They're even worse. There's no chance of skipping your homework.'

Mum was still out shopping when we arrived back home so Andy and I told Grandma our plan. She looked in the *Yellow Pages* and sure enough there was a Wildlife Centre near where Charles Anderson lived.

'We'll give it a try,' whispered Grandma as she heard Mum's key in the door. 'Next Saturday we'll set out on "Operation Boyfriend – the last chance!" '

33

The week started with Grandma getting another letter from Australia. I picked it up from the mat and looked at it. It had a koala stamp on it, but, before I could examine it further, Grandma appeared, took it from me and stuffed it in her dressing-gown pocket.

'Another letter from your pen pal,' I said, giving Grandma the chance to tell me all about it.

'Yes,' was all she said.

'Your *pen pal* writes quite a lot now,' I said.

'Yes.'

'Must have a lot of news.'

'Some.'

'Why do you never write back?' I asked.

'Why do you ask so many questions?' said Grandma.

And that was that. She took her letter to her room and said no more, so I had to take my curiosity elsewhere. I took it to Mum in the kitchen. She was in a rush to get to work so the conversation was a bit odd.

'Grandma's got another letter from her pen pal in Australia.'

'Now where did I put my car keys?'

'Do you know who the pen pal is?'

'I was sure they were in my handbag.'

'Do you know why Grandma never writes back?'

'Maybe they're in my jacket pocket.'

'Three slimy green aliens from the planet Mucus have landed in the back garden and are now eating next door's cat. Miaow. Miaow. Mia—'

'Got them. Hurry up or you'll miss the school bus, Abby. See you tonight.'

Mum left, banging the front door behind her. Ever get the feeling your parents never listen to a word you say?

I mentioned this to Velvet in school when we were supposed to be looking at the poems of Wilfred Owen.

'My mum's the same,' said Velvet. 'She only hears what she wants to hear. Requests for more pocket money or a new CD player haven't a hope.'

'Hmm, selective deafness,' I said. 'Maybe it goes with having children.'

'Abigail Montgomery,' snapped Mrs Jackson, 'will you stop chatting and get on with reading *Greater Love*. What is so important anyway, that you have to talk about it now? Friday night's disco, I expect.'

'No, it wasn't,' I said truthfully. 'I was discussing the possibility of selective deafness being a side effect of motherhood.'

Mrs Jackson gave me a hard stare.

'Get on with your work,' she said.

I worked hard for the rest of the day – double Maths is really difficult when you haven't a clue what the teacher's on about – but at least, at the end of the day, I got to take home my efforts from Technical. We'd been doing Metalwork that term and I had the choice of making either a shoehorn or a trowel. You only ever see shoehorns in shoe shops so I'd decided to make Mum a trowel she could use in the garden. I'd quite enjoyed doing it, and now that I'd finished smoothing off the edges, Mr Forbes, the Technical teacher, said I could take it home.

I thought about keeping it for Mum's Christmas present, but I knew she'd really prefer smelly soap, so I gave her the trowel as soon as she got in from work.

'Present for you,' I said. 'I made it in Tech. I thought you might find it useful.'

'Oh I will,' she said. 'It's lovely, thank you. I've never had a . . . shoehorn before. You usually only see them in shoe shops.'

I said nothing.

But while Mum was in a good mood, having been given the trowel/shoehorn pressie, I brought up the subject of the visit to the Wildlife Centre.

'Andy and I are really keen to go, and it would help with my Biology project next term.'

'Well, I don't know . . .'

Mum was at it again.

Grandma weighed in. 'Tell you what,' she said, 'why don't I go with them, Eva? I'd like to see the Wildlife Centre too, and I could keep an eye on them.'

'And they could keep an eye on you.'

Grandma and I both took that as a 'yes'.

'Good, that's settled then,' we both said.

Mum's eyes narrowed. She knew she'd been outmanoeuvred.

'Just make sure you two behave. I don't want to have to tell Andy's mother he's in jail.'

We both made a 'Don't be ridiculous' face.

Mum frowned. 'Sometimes you two are so alike. No wonder I worry.'

'I've contacted Charles Anderson,' Grandma whispered to me later. 'He's a professor of English at the university, and has invited us all there for afternoon tea on Saturday.'

'Wow,' I said. 'Professor of English. I wonder if he'll speak using really big words. Perhaps I'd better try to collect a few more before the weekend.'

'We'll set off early,' said Grandma. 'That way we can go to the Wildlife Centre first. Your mum's bound to ask about it.'

'You're right,' I said. 'Good thinking, Grandma.'

34

Have you ever noticed how slowly the weekdays seem to pass when you've something exciting to do at the weekend? That week was no exception. Monday plodded into Tuesday. Tuesday limped into Wednesday. Wednesday crept into Thursday. Thursday dragged into Friday. And Friday... well, I went to bed early on Friday just so Saturday would finally get here. Then, would you believe it, I slept in and had to scurry for the train.

Andy was on the platform looking anxiously at his watch as Grandma and I panted up.

'I'm getting too old for this,' puffed Grandma.

'Me too,' I said. 'I was starting to limp!' Then I looked down at my feet and realized why. I had on two odd shoes with different heel heights.

'Fashion statement?' grinned Andy.

'Little mistake,' grinned Grandma.

!!++! I thought. I had wanted to impress the professor too. Perhaps we could buy some shoes somewhere. But by the time we had bought our train tickets and paid our admission to the Wildlife Centre, the only footwear we could have afforded was wellies, and it wasn't raining. I continued to limp.

The Wildlife Centre was great. We enthused over the long-tailed lemurs, exclaimed over the Bengal tigers, and sat down exhausted to watch the penguins at feeding time.

Grandma produced some Coke and sandwiches and we had our own version of feeding time. Not so spectacular as swallowing fish whole, but just as effective. When the last sandwich had been scoffed, Andy and I did a penguin waddle to the nearest bin with our litter.

'Why is that big girl wearing different shoes?' asked a small child, face almost hidden behind an enormous ice cream.

'I expect she has another pair the same at home,' said his mum.

Some people think they are so funny.

Grandma looked at her watch. 'Time to go and visit the professor,' she said.

We took a bus to the university and admired the old buildings as the bus took us up University Avenue. The English department was in an ivy-clad building in a tree-lined quadrangle. It looked so old and impressive I was quite overawed. Andy felt the same. Grandma wasn't bothered.

'I used to come here to student dances in the sixties,' she said. 'See that window over there?'

She pointed to a low window with leaded glass in a corner of the building. 'That leads into a cloakroom. If you hadn't enough money for a dance ticket, someone would let you in through that window. I tried it once, but fell through on the other side and took the knees out of my tights.'

I grinned. Good old Grandma. Now I wasn't quite so upset by my odd shoes.

Grandma gave our names to the porter and he called the professor to say we had arrived. Two minutes later, a middle-sized man with a shock of white hair came down the wide stone stairs and into the big stone hall to meet us.

'Aphrodite!' he cried, hugging Grandma. 'How wonderful to see you after all this time. Your name's still Aphrodite, I take it. You haven't changed it back again?'

WHAT???

My eyebrows shot up into my hairline, and I looked at Grandma. She gave me one of her 'Don't ask now, I'll explain later' looks, and said, 'No, it's still Aphrodite. How are you, Charlie? You look good.'

'Well, I'm older and not much wiser,' grinned the professor. Then he turned to me.

'This must be your granddaughter,' he said. 'She looks so like you.'

I smiled, giving him the full benefit of my dental work.

'This is my friend, Andy,' I said. 'We're delighted to meet you.'

Now didn't that sound grown-up? I'd been secretly practising it on the bus.

The professor led us up the wide stone staircase to his study. 'Sit down and we'll have some tea,' he said. 'I've got a packet of chocolate biscuits somewhere.'

He poked about among some books and unearthed a packet of Blue Ribands.

'They always were your favourite, Charlie,' laughed Grandma. 'You haven't changed a bit.'

After that the two of them started off down memory lane. They were like a couple of kids, giggling and laughing. Andy and I looked at each other and helped ourselves to another chocolate biscuit. Then we stood up and wandered round the room. The study was amazing. Wall-to-wall books. Floor-to-ceiling books, almost. I had a look in some of them. Wow, I'd have to collect a few more words before I could even begin to understand them. No pictures in them either. The professor must have read my mind for he looked over and said, 'On top of that pile of books on the table there, you'll find one you might enjoy. It's by my son.'

I found a large book by David Anderson and opened it. It was full of cartoons. They were brilliant. Really funny.

'My son's a wonderful cartoonist,' said the professor proudly. 'He's won prizes for his work. That's just a small collection of some of his drawings.'

'They're fantastic,' I said, and Andy and I sat on

the carpet with the book between us and giggled over them for ages.

It also answered one question – the prof had a son. The next question was up to Grandma and she came straight out with it. 'Is your son married?' she asked.

'Was,' said the prof. 'He has a son, probably about Abby's age.'

'Does he live far away?' Grandma was doing well with the questions.

The prof shook his head. 'Half an hour by car, five minutes if you walk.'

Grandma laughed and they got on to talking about how much worse the traffic was nowadays. Honestly, you'd have thought the wheel had hardly been invented when they were young.

After another cup of tea and no more biscuits – Andy and I had scoffed the lot – it was time to go.

'We must keep in touch now, Charlie,' said Grandma. 'Would you and your son and grandson come to tea with us next Saturday? I'd like your son to meet my daughter.'

'What a good idea,' said the professor. 'I'm always telling David he should get out more and meet people. He gets stuck behind that drawing board and forgets there's a big world out there.'

'Right,' beamed Grandma, 'that's settled then. Our house next Saturday at three o'clock.'

'I'll look forward to it,' said the professor.

Me too, I thought. This should be interesting . . .

35

Grandma and I parted from Andy at the station and made our way home.

'Had a good day?' asked Mum, as I quickly slipped out of my odd shoes and padded round in my socks.

'Great,' said Grandma. 'The Wildlife Centre was superb. You should go some time. Then I met an old friend, Charlie Anderson, from my student days. He's a professor of English at the university. We had afternoon tea with him, and I've invited him and his family here for afternoon tea next Saturday. I hope that's all right.'

I listened and learned. Grandma had told the truth without telling the truth. She had just left out the bits that would upset Mum. Like how we'd planned the whole thing.

But Mum wasn't that much of a pushover.

'Your old friend and his *family*?' she asked.

Grandma nodded, all innocent.

'What family does he have?'

'A son and a grandson, I think. I'm not exactly sure.'

Mum's eyes narrowed.

'Does the son have a wife or a partner?'

'Not exactly sure of that either,' Grandma was stalling.

'Shall I make us some tea?' I asked, brightly, hoping to create a diversion.

'In a minute,' frowned Mum. 'This wouldn't be another of your little ploys to find me a man?' she asked.

Grandma looked injured. 'You told me not to do that.'

'Exactly,' said Mum. 'Well, your friends are very welcome to come to tea, but I won't be here. I'll be out doing the shopping as usual.'

'You can't do that!' protested Grandma. 'I've told Charlie all about you, and he's really keen to meet you. You can't disappear off. I didn't bring you up to be rude.'

Mum looked thoughtful. 'You're right,' she said. 'It would be impolite not to be here. OK, I'll meet them.'

And that was that. She went off humming to put the kettle on.

'I don't like it,' Grandma whispered to me. 'She's up to something.'

'She's not the only one,' I said. 'So are you. What was all that business earlier about your name?'

Grandma grinned. 'Do you like your name, Abby?'

148

I shrugged. 'It's all right, though sometimes I think about spelling it A-B-I or A-B-B-I just to be different. I get cross if we're doing a poem in class that's got an abbey in it and everyone laughs and points. But it could be worse. There's a girl in the year above called Annette Curtin and Andy's got a cousin called Robin Hood.'

Grandma nodded. 'I just didn't like the name I'd been given at birth. I didn't feel it suited me, so I changed it.'

'What were you called?' I asked. 'Was it something awful like Walburga or Zenobia?' I'd found these names in my dictionary recently when I'd been looking up the meaning of a word for my collection.

'Worse than that,' said Grandma. 'It was Agnes.'

'Agnes? That's not too bad. What's wrong with Agnes?'

'Nothing, except it just wasn't me. I don't look like an Agnes. I don't act like an Agnes. Agnes is a sensible name for a sensible person. It just didn't suit me.'

She had a point. I loved my grandma dearly, but sensible she wasn't.

'Fair enough,' I said, 'but why Aphrodite?'

'She was the Greek goddess of love and beauty. With a name like that no one ever forgets who you are. What more can I say?'

Not a lot!

'Actually, there is something else I have to tell

you,' Grandma went on. 'But first you might want to ask your mum about *her* name.'

Curiouser and curiouser. I headed for the kitchen. Mum was just dunking the tea bags into the mugs.

'Is there something funny about your name?' I asked. 'I've just found out Grandma's real name is Agnes. Isn't Eva your real name? If not, what is?'

Mum went a bit pink, sploshed some milk into the mugs and sighed.

'Promise you won't laugh,' she said.

I promised.

'Godiva.'

I laughed.

'See?' said Mum. 'You laughed, and so did everyone else when I was at school. That's why I changed it.'

'But why on earth did Grandma call you Godiva? Wasn't she the woman that was supposed to have ridden naked through the streets of Coventry?'

'To secure a promise from her husband, Leofric, Earl of Mercia, that he would reduce taxation,' said Grandma, coming in to collect her tea. 'She was an English heroine. Her name means a divine gift. That's what I thought your mother was when she was born so I wanted to give her a memorable name.'

'It was memorable all right,' said Mum. 'No one ever forgot it. It's taken me this long to try to live it down.'

I looked at them and shook my head. Whatever else Grandma had to tell couldn't be any more off the wall than this.

But it was.

'OK, Grandma,' I said. 'You mentioned there was something else you had to tell me. It's not that the tooth fairy's really my mum, is it? Because I had that sussed at least three months ago.'

'No, it's not that,' smiled Grandma, and looked a bit uncomfortable.

'What then?' asked Mum and I together.

'Well,' said Grandma. 'You know I told you Handsome Harris fell into the sheep dip and drowned?'

'Yes?'

'Well . . . he didn't.'

'He didn't fall into the sheep dip?' frowned Mum.

'He didn't drown?' I said.

Grandma shook her head.

'So what . . .' we both said.

'He's still alive,' said Grandma. 'We just pretended he was dead.'

Mum sank down on to a kitchen chair.

'Why?' she said. 'And this had better be good.'

'Well,' said Grandma. 'You know I said Handsome Harris wasn't very good about paying bills and taxes and things. I'm afraid he got himself into a bit of a muddle and had to borrow money from some crooks to pay off his debts. But then the crooks wanted to be paid back too, but much more than they'd originally said. I suppose that's because they're crooks. There wasn't enough money from the sale of the sheep farm, so we decided I would come back home and Handsome would disappear for a while, till the heat was off.'

'Till the heat was off?' screeched Mum. 'It's sounds like something out of an old gangster movie!'

'So that's who your letters were from then,' I cried.

Grandma nodded. 'Handsome started to write once he thought the coast was clear. Once he thought he'd given the crooks the slip. Once he thought they'd stopped chasing him.'

Mum put her head in her hands.

'I'm hoping to be made a partner in the firm and I discover my mother is married to a raised-from-the-dead tax evader, who is being chased all over the outback by the Australian mafia. What am I going to do?'

'Nothing, Eva,' said Grandma. 'You worry too much. Just let matters take their natural course. They'll be right.'

I looked at them both. What a pair. Grandma was doing her best to be cheerful. Mum looked like it was the last day at breakfast. I had to do something to rescue the situation, so I grabbed a banana from the fruit bowl, scratched a bit and swung on the kitchen door. Mum and Grandma were so surprised they forgot themselves long enough to burst out laughing.

I grinned and made my teeth chatter. Thank goodness for my monkey impression. It can always be relied upon to help out in sticky moments.

36

Grandma and I spent the week worrying and wondering about the meeting on Saturday, and how it would go.

'We mustn't get our hopes up too much, Abby,' said Grandma. 'We haven't even seen Charlie's son. He may be horrible. Your mum may dislike him on sight.'

'Not if he's anything like Charlie,' I said. 'I liked him. He's nice. Didn't you fancy him when you were young, Grandma?'

'Oh yes,' grinned Grandma, 'but I fancied your grandad more.'

'And then there was Handsome Harris.'

'And then there was Handsome Harris,' she agreed.

Grandma was quiet for a moment then was suddenly brisk. 'Now what shall we have for our Saturday afternoon tea? Blue Ribands, of course . . .'

'And KitKats. I like them. So does Andy. It's a pity he can't be here, but it's his gran's birthday and the family are taking her out for the day. Oh, and we'd better have an apple tart. That's Mum's favourite, and always puts her in a good mood.'

So it was settled. Grandma did the shopping, and I helped to tidy up. I even tidied away Mum's books. Really, parents can be *so* messy sometimes. By two-forty-five on the following Saturday afternoon, the house was spic-and-span, and Grandma and I were as neat and tidy as we would ever be. I wore matching shoes and Grandma had on her best jeans. We waited for Mum to come downstairs as she'd just gone up to change.

She'd changed all right. Not into the nice little frock Grandma had suggested, nor into the jeans and polo neck that I had suggested, but into her saggy tracky bottoms and old faded Wombles T-shirt. Her favourite programme when she'd been little.

'What on earth?' said Grandma.

'What are you doing, Mum?' I said. 'The visitors will be here soon!'

'I know,' said Mum sweetly. 'I've just got time to start creosoting the shed before they arrive.'

She picked up a large paintbrush and a tin of smelly creosote and went out into the garden.

Grandma and I looked at each other, aghast.

'I knew she was up to something,' muttered Grandma. 'She always was a tricky child.'

'What are we going to do?' I said. 'They'll be here soon.'

Grandma looked out of the window. 'Nothing we can do. It's too late. They're here now.'

Grandma opened the front door and Professor Charlie came in with his son and his grandson. The prof and his grandson looked a bit uncomfortable, but his son was very cheerful.

'Hi,' he said. 'I'm David Anderson. How nice of you to invite us.'

I burst out laughing. I couldn't help it, for while the prof and his grandson had, like Grandma and I, got decently dressed for the afternoon, his son, David, was in paint-splashed old jeans and a washed-out rugby top.

'What's so funny?' he said.

'Nothing,' I grinned. 'Come and meet Mum. She's creosoting the shed.'

I took them all out to the back garden. Mum had started on the front of the shed, and on the front of herself. Madame Cholé now had a fetching brown tan and Great Uncle Bulgaria would never be able to read his *Times* again.

Mum and David looked at each other, and at their outfits.

'Snap,' they both said, and laughed.

'Children!' sighed Grandma and Charlie.

'Parents!' sighed Mum and David.

'Fancy a KitKat?' I said to the grandson, Peter, and over several we swopped stories. His dad had been equally suspicious of the afternoon invitation and had refused to get 'properly' dressed too.

'Grown-ups,' we agreed. 'What a pain.'

But it turned out fine in the end. Everyone got on so well that Charlie, David and Peter stayed on for dinner. We got Chinese carry-outs. Mum and David both liked sweet and sour chicken.

It was a really good day and we were all sorry to see it end. Even Mum. *Especially* Mum. I could be wrong, but I thought she looked younger, and had more colour in her cheeks, though that could have been the white wine she and David shared.

After the guests had gone, we were clearing away the last of the take-away cartons when I asked her.

'Well?' I said. 'Well?'

'Well what?' she grinned.

'You know what,' I said. 'Did David ask you out? You were giggling and talking so much something must have happened.'

'Mind your own business,' said Mum, but she was smiling so much I was sure we'd be seeing more of David. That was good. I liked him, and Charlie and Peter. It would be nice to have some men around the house for a change.

When I went to bed that night I thought over all the things that had gone on since Grandma'd come to stay: Benson, the school bus, getting arrested and of course, Operation Boyfriend. More had happened in the six months she'd been here than I could remember in all the previous years of my existence. It was great.

'I hope she stays,' I yawned. 'I hope one day I get to meet Handsome Harris. I hope the Australian mafia don't get him. I wonder what they look like. I bet they wear suits with fat pinstripes and hats with dangling champagne corks. I bet they have mafia molls in tight spangly dresses and matching nail polish. And I bet they all look like Belinda Fishcake.'